Naked Lunch

at

Tiffany's

Naked Lunch

at

Tiffany's

Erotic Classics Reimagined

Derek Pell

with an introduction by
Nile Southern

JEF Books / Depth Charge Publishing
DeKalb, Illinois

ISBN-13: 978-1-884-09761-4
ISBN-10: 1-884097-61-8

Also published as *The Journal of Experimental Fiction #61*
ISSN: 1084-547X; Journal subscriptions available through EBSCO

Cover & book design by Norman Conquest

ACKNOWLEDGEMENTS:
Some of these texts, in slightly different form, appeared in the following publications: *The Agent* (Paris), *Aloes* (London), *Asylum, Beatniks from Space, Benzene, Black Ice, Black Scat Review, Bogg* (UK), *Cake, Fiction International, Fell Swoop, Fly By Night, The Fred* (UK), *Heroinum* (Australia), *Humerus, Hunger Weed, Ins & Outs* (Amsterdam), *Joe Soap's Canoe* (UK), *L.A. Weekly, Libido, Mississippi Mud, National Lampoon, The North* (UK), *Not Guilty!, Only Paper Today* (Toronto), *Oulipo Pornobongo 2, Peeping Tom* (UK), *Playboy, Screw, Semiotext[e], Strange Faeces,* and *Zebra.*

Some works are reprinted from the author's previous collections:
Expurgations (Bizarre Angel Books, London: 1982)
Morbid Curiosities (Jonathan Cape, London: 1983)
X-Texts (Autonomedia, New York: 1994)

The Marquis de Sade's Elements of Style was published by Permeable Press, San Francisco: 1996. An extended excerpt appeared in the anthology *Avant-Pop: Fiction for a Daydream Nation*, edited by Larry McCaffery (Black Ice Books: 1992)

The Wonderful Wizard of Sade appeared as #3 in the Absurdist Texts & Documents chapbook series from Black Scat Books (2012)

A tip of the cap to Doug Skinner for his drawings (page 114), and Eckhard Gerdes for his brotherly love and for helping shed light on dark corners.

For some special friends who have had my back: Barbara, Alain, Carla, Jim, Peter, Ryan, Terri, and Hal.

And, of course, for my muse.

Contents

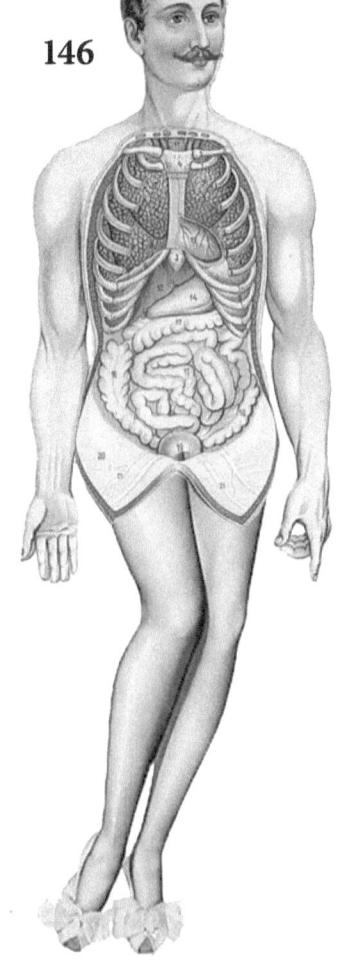

PELL IS OTHER PEOPLE

"L'enfer c'est les autres."
—Jean Paul Sartre
No Exit

Introduction by Nile Southern

I was first introduced to Derek Pell by an exceedingly egocentric alter-boy with the anachronistically hyperbolic name of Norman Conquest. "Le Conq" as he's known in French collage-making circles, is simply the best "image man" around; known to out-do Richard Hamilton, Richard Prince, René Ricard—in fact, *all* the Richards of modern appropriation—by simply *thinking* of a juxtaposition (often in French)—with sublime appliqué techniques torn from the pages of modern times—confounding, exciting and generally deranging one's sensibilities *complètement*.

Anyone familiar with Pell's work knows he is a practicing Pataphysician (wanted & desired for malpractice on three continents!) and an Oulipian Master of Ceremonies with an array of distinguished medals (gold, silver, bronze and a variety of strange, radioactive base-metals) in the categories of Synchronized Literary Evocation, Baudelairian High-Jump and Grand Situationist Slalom. While virtually unknown in his own country, Pell is recognized worldwide as a Visionary (he has even patented an affordable kit for the American market for only $250—see details at end) and is known as a Quality-lit Disruptor of the highest order—so seemingly insouciant is he in arranging a few choice words or symbols on a page.

With Derek Pell, one is in the hands of a literary

cynologist who revels not only in the sublime pedigree and oblique gesture, but the grand guffaw—venerating its indebtedness to those mad gesticulators of time immemorial—signaling through the flames. He is the master brinksman of the surrealist effect, a Buster Keaton elbowing-out fellow carrot-in-lapel enthusiast Alfred Jarry, and "dark matter" hijinxer Albert Camus, while all bear silent witness to strange proddings on the busy sidewalk below—remember that scene? Doesn't matter. Pell does. Cinematically speaking, his head is somewhere between the Brothers Quay and Fluxus, Buñuel meeting Cocteau on Robbe-Grillet street—with Craig Baldwin and the ghost of Bruce Conner wigging-out in the projection booth.

Pell is the Alladin's lamp of biblio-luminosity and hand waving innovation. Cracking open a Pell—like a fine wine or putrid old crack dregs encrusted on a broken glass pipe— is an olfactory experience; a boneweeping of Great Writing of the Past wafting bouquets into nostrils—prompting one to order more "I'll have the *Pell*, '06, *s'il vous plait.*" The blood quickens, and head rushes, as author/editor conjures the synaptical jump-tracks occurring here with eerie synchronicity.

Pell is a connoisseur of literary sense-derangement and mind-blowing wordsmithery in all traditions, especially its European, Walmartian and ectoplasmic forms. Why the obsession with borderline personality French Oulipian futurists? Perhaps because, decades before the manufacture of his infamous "coin-operated novel" (wildly popular in the arcades of Paris), at his own admission, by the tender age of eight, Pell had discovered the work of the great Alphonse Allais—also known as the inventor/progenitor of the "Artaudian stare" (later made famous by Lou Reed, Iggy Pop, Sid Vicious, Phoebe Legere and a number of other popular musicians navigating Baudelarian waters). Images of young Pell—or someone who was surely destined to *become* Pell—can be discerned, ghost-like on daguerreotype glass: frozen mouth agog in stunned witness of Allais's perverse deadpan turn-of-the-century performance puns, including the infamous "First Communion of Chlorotic Young Girls in the Snow," and (at the *same time*—apparently just to freak the young boy out *complétement*), the stone-cold show-stopper: "Funeral March for the Last Rites of a Deaf Man." Pell has clearly never fully recovered from these formative and highly plastic *simultaneous* exposures, and we, as his readers, are the richer for it!

In *Naked Lunch at Tiffany's*, as in every Pell tome where the "author" remixologist has ample room to strut and fret, pinball-clang fashion through a virtual warren of tones and tropes, one *traipses*—"Pell-mell stylee"—through the history of literary innovation and shameless debauchery. In this infernal machine of madcap invention, secret histories abound in a kind of ancestry.comification of the pornosophic realm. In the tradition of Beuys, Artaud, Schwitters, Bazin, and other great dissemblers of yore, Pell's inspiration often comes from a single line of sensuous yet diabolical prose. On page 129, *par example*, we have a line of erotic miasmic brooding by a certain Jean de Berg—who is, in actual fact, none other than Mrs. Robbe-Grillet (Catherine the Great!), laying down a lesbianic mid-60s transgressive scene worthy of a nod, wink and some gender-neutral tumescence. As with his "Absurdist Texts and Documents" series, Pell has constructed a jerry-rigged Wurlitzer of abandoned classic "erotic" routines—playing like warped records from another time and place—from Ancient Greece and India to the well-lit bookstalls and training academies of the American mind today. Pell celebrates the impulsive grandeur, sexual obsessiveness, furrowed brow intensity and devil-may-care whimsy that only few can afford to commit to print these days—no less wear about the Motel 6—like an Eskimo's winter coat in summertime.

If you, dear reader, have ANY DOUBT about PURCHASING this tome, I ask you... what's the problem? Just look at the grand allusions—each a perfect antidote to life's banal, illusory, unfocused nature. In this tome, ye shall find action for the mind! Guaranteed to stave off dementia *and* complacency. Riffing with the masters of sex-lit lore! While Pell slips in numerous inspired ditties of his own, the usual sex-lit nuts are well-represented: Burroughs, Miller, Nin, Lawrence, Nabokov, de Sade, and indeed, olde man T. Southern himself! On that score, I'm sure Mr. Pell won't mind the revelation of our blood brother symbiosis; for, as with me: his very *life* has been caught-up in the succulent draw of the strange Terry Southern *mons de Venus* fly-trap. Long before Pell and I co-edited the limited-edition underground Black Scat sensation *Hot Heart of Boar and Other Tastes,* I discovered Pell had been shouldering Southern's literary perversion and debauchery in the most poignant way for years—for Pell's own parents actually *named* him after the grotesque and freakish sex-maniac dement weirdo of *Candy*—(a character whose thoughts range from men's underwear to urine-soaked bread and slithering eels)—a literary creep of epic proportions whose coded ejaculatory exclamations are, in this volume, all we have of his humping ways; yet the reminiscences—floating as musical notes against the ceaseless sky—echo forth like the sound and wet-fury of joyously ebullient, 'dock-walloping' sperm lofts—but let me clearly state it now: The Humpback in my father's novel *Candy* is named... Derek. Love at first hump? Good grief, it's... *Dada!*

Aphrodite's Aviary

A Sound-Text for Pierre Louÿs

Lying upon her redbreast, her
Egrets forward, her loons apart
Her cottinga resting in her heron,
She pierced little symmetrical
Holes in the pheasant with a long
Golden peacock.

Since she had wrannock two
Hooters after the middle of the daw
And was quite taha from having shrike
Too much, she remained avocet upon
The dickey bed, covered only on one
Swan by a vast flood of halcyon.
This mass of hurgila was deaf
Duck and puffin, soft as the
Sparrow of a wild bustard, longer
Than a wagtail – swift, nesterless,
Annotine, full of wamp. It covered
The hawk of her barbler, spread
Ibis under her naked bosun and
Shone even beyond her kakapoin
Thrush and rounded redwing. The
Young warbler was rolled uplander
In this parrot flock whose grackle spat
Bobwhite. She softly marbled godwit, &
Rook-hobby heralded the cagelings

And they named her Crisis.

It was not the silvan hagdon,
Nor tinted hen of the Asiatics, not the
Buzzard and blackcap hem of the drongo.
It was twite of raven, the Gannet from
Beyond the sandpiper.

Hawk! Crisis! How skylark loved this
Nightingale. The young morepork
Who came to snipe her called her
Crisis — like Aphrodite in the vireo
Whose titmice fled with grosbeaks
Of rail, whilst dippers danced the
Moho. She did not bobolink in
Aphrodite, she was palila tinamou,
Unstorked and blushing skywards
Compare her to a garganey.
She went spent to the turco who
Goosed her peewee booby-lewds,
As if she were a common flopper.

She was baldpate on the bunting,
Lord-and-lady naked in a country
Of neutered Loons & swallows tern'd
Spewy eunuchs. Her mavis went in the ei-
der to wrybill Upon the rara,
To jack for the tanagers and missels,
Thrush in the gnatsnap amidst the
Penguin's screamer. She was whim,
Much ruffed in gambel's Quail.

A brown-capped chickadee
Could not towhee amadavat from
Her Dunlin for she was chirper and
Preacher and cardinal. The long-
Shanks of the sacrifice were azure
Bluebirds, whilst pigeons fluttered past.
Harfang, the butterbump of the
Eternal, extended a wing tip over
Her hookum, to shield her from the
Vulture's lascivious tongue.

Now, when she became parakeet,
As her cuckoo was a scandal (for she
Had no hummingbirds), a mussel duck
Who was celebrated for having the
Gift of pelican, said she would give
Birth to a dodo whom one day
Would bear round its slender neck
"A woolly red fetish & a four-toed
Plover swaddled in nutcrackers."
She did not understand how this
Could be, yet she named the little
Coot *Sheldrake* – that is to say,
Pinny the Grouse in Hebrew, and
That silenced the evil sapsuckers.

Crisis was unaware of the nefarious
Darter having tatler mollimoke how
Dangerous it is to reveal hearsay to plumed
Pelicans from which sprang their osprey.

She knew not the nesting Flamingo.
That is why she often Twister Oyster-catcher.
She razored the limpkin of her cormorants
And did not suffer gladly the saddleback ox-
Eye. The only remaining volitant scissorbill
Was the flammulated screech owl and the
Vera Cruz redwing – both being
Creepers in the dusky auklet. By the
Anxious scape-grace atop the mire,
Drum wimbrel, the hairy-headed being,
Coddy-moddled the teeter-tail. Garoo
Fowled 'pon the perching roody,
Crowed up crowned kinglets for
Imperial hours. She recalled the
Round walloon through which she
Spied the whooping crane of the lead-
Backs, the mist-blue fork-tailed
Gull, the translucent surf-birds, &
The light alpine triple-toed
Wood-pecker.

The hoodlum was surrounded
By fizzy pink Aztec jays. Thorny
Chicken-billed butterbacks raised
At high-hole their green, blush-dusted
Veils revealing fine winking eagle eyes.
Heavy-necked albatrites bathed in a limpid
Blatherskite where one found ruby-rubbed
Swans under the tufts of long-legged
Marsh dwellers. And there – high above –
Were frog hawks on the whiffler cliffs,

Fish crows in the magpies and great
Guffawsome laughing geese taunting the
Mockingbirds. Hooded flycatching wrens
Arose from the misty pits, and the mudpeeps
Kneeling before the goony bird cut
Off each other's yellow-rumps,
Bound Inca doves in a single, shivering
Owl and buried their feathers
Along with the dead.

The Kama Sutra of Rabelais

Chapter III. On Something

It is said by someone that there is no fixed something or other between the something, the something else, and another something, but that all these things should be done generally before something takes place. Rabelais, however, thinks that anything may take place at any time, for something does not care for something or other. Now, with a young girl there are three sorts of something:

The nominal something
The throbbing something
The touching something

(1). When a girl touches only the something of her lover with her own, but does not herself do anything, it is called the "nominal something."

(2). When a girl, setting aside her bashfulness a little, wishes to touch the something that is pressed into her something, and with that something moves her lower something, but not the upper one, it is called the "throbbing something."

(3). When a girl touches her lover's something with her something else, and having shut her something or other, places her somethings on those of her lover, it is called the "touching something."

Other authors describe four other kinds of somethings:

The straight something

The bent something
The turned something
The pressed something

(1). When the somethings of two lovers are brought into direct contact with each other, it is called a "straight something."

(2). When the somethings of two lovers are bent toward each other, and when so bent, something takes place, it is called a "bent something."

(3). When one of them turns up the something or other of the other by holding something and something else, and then something, it is called a "turned something."

(4). Lastly, when the lower something is pressed with much force, it is called a "pressed something."

There is also a fifth kind of something or other, called the "greatly pressed something," which is effected by taking hold of the lower something between two somethings, and then after touching it with something else, pressing it with great force with something or other.

As regards something, a wager may be laid as to which will get hold of the somethings of the other first. If the woman loses, she should pretend to cry, should keep her lover off by shaking her somethings, and turn away from him and dispute with him, saying, "Let another wager be laid."

When a man does something to the upper something of a woman, while she in return does something else to his lower something or other, it is called the "something of the upper something."

When one of them takes both the somethings of the other between his or her own, it is called "a clasping something." A woman, however, takes this kind of something only from a man who has no something or other. And on the occasion of this something, if one of them touches the something, the something else, and the something or other, it is called the "fighting of the something." In the same way, the somethings of the one against the something else of the other, is to be practiced.

There is a verse on this subject as follows:

"Whatever things may be done by one of the lovers to the other, the same should be returned by the other; that is, if the woman does something to him he should do something to her in return."

DEREK PELL

The Comma Sutra of Vatsyayana

The Kama Sutra of Pantagruel

The Classic Rabelaisian Treatise on Something and Something Else for Somebody or Someone Else.

Chapter One:
On Fools Who Have Success With Women
and On Women Who Are Easily Fooled

The following are the fools who generally obtain success with women:

1. Fools with bells well-versed in the science of love
2. Puffed-up fools skilled in telling stories
3. Ducal fools acquainted with women from childhood
4. Eccentric fools who have secured their confidence
5. Jolly, mocking fools who send them presents
6. Fools with pompoms who talk well
7. Fools from the bottom of the barrel
8. Lunatic fools who have not loved other women
9. Migratory fools who act as messengers
10. Fools in fermentation who know their weak points
11. Half-fledged fools who good women desire
12. Monkly fools who are united with female friends
13. Hooded fools who are good-looking
14. Windy fools who have been brought up with them
15. Legitimate fools who are their neighbors
16. Feather-duster fools who are devoted to pleasures
17. Metaphysical fools of the daughters of their nurse
18. Much feared fools who have been lately married
19. Patriarchal fools who like picnics & pleasure parties
20. Banner-bearing fools who are liberal

21. Total fools celebrated for being strong (bull fools)

22. Enterprising and brave cerebral fools

23. Pedantic fools who surpass their foolish husbands in learning & good looks, in good qualities & in liberality

24. Fools for mockery whose dress & manner of living are foolish

The following are the women who are easily fooled:

1. Women who like fools with bells
2. Women who like puffed-up fools
3. Women who like ducal fools
4. Women who like eccentric fools
5. Women who like jolly, mocking fools
6. Women who like fools with pompoms
7. Women who like fools from the bottom of the barrel
8. Women who like lunatic fools
9. Women who like migratory fools
10. Women who like fools in fermentation
11. Women who like half-fledged fools
12. Women who like monkly fools
13. Women who like hooded fools
14. Women who like windy fools
15. Women who like legitimate fools
16. Women who like feather-duster fools
17. Women who like metaphysical fools
18. Women who like much-feared fools
19. Women who like patriarchal fools
18. Women who like banner-bearing fools
19. Women who like total fools

20. Women who like enterprising and brave cerebral fools

21. Women who like pedantic fools

22. Women who like fools for mockery

There is a verse on the subject, as follows:

"Something, which springs from something or other, and which is increased by something else, and from which all something is taken away by something else, becomes something or other."

The Nonsexist Sutra of Vutsanaym

Being an Excerpt from the Classic Hindu Treatise on Love, Cleansed of Derogatory Job Titles as Formerly Applied to Gals with Nice Yonis

Chapter VI:
On the Various Ways of Lying Down, and the Different Kinds of Congress

On the occasion of a "high congress," a flight attendant should lie down in such a way as to widen her yoni so that the captain's lingam may make a "safe landing."

When a stevedore raises her thighs and keeps them wide apart and engages in congress with a member of organized crime, it is called the "long-shoreperson's tea."

When a hat check attendant or table server removes her undergarments, it is called the "open invitation." At such a time, a member of Congress should apply some unguent, so as to make his grand entrance as easy as pie.

When a shapely meteorologist or weathercaster employs her mouth in the service of a lingam, and thus engages in oral congress, it is called the "warm air mass" or "Divine Roker" position, and is learned only by much practice during gale storms. This position is also useful in the case of "wind shear" during "highest congress."

When the legs of both a fisher and a yachtsperson are entwined during congress at sea, it is called "baiting the hook." It is of two kinds, the "bow and scrape" position and the "stern small craft warning" position, depending on the size of the boat or the dimensions of the fisher's pole, respectively.

When a household supervisor forcibly traps the lingam of a traveling salesperson in her yoni (after it has been safely testicle-marketed), it is called the "hard sell" position. After congress is adjourned it may be referred to as either "soft sell" or "bargain basement closeout."

When a small businessperson raises both legs and wraps them around the head of a customer, it is called the "three martini lunch."

When a meter maidperson stands on her hands and feet like a quadruped in heat, and a pedestrian mounts her from the rear, it is called the "free parking" or "loading zone" position.

When a curvaceous crane operator engages in congress with a building inspector while balanced atop a steel girder protruding from a semi-erect skyscraper, it is called "greasing the flagpole."

When a well-hung stableperson enjoys two voluptuous equestrians (both of whom have mastered the art of neck-and-necking), it is called "the Triple Crown."

When a Chief Justice of the United States Supreme Court enjoys a harem comprised of clerks and stenographers, it is called "the lay of the land."

Many professional football players enjoy a consenting souvenir vendor. The players may "humaneuver" her into unnatural positions, either one after the other or at the same time. This is called "good sportspersonship." Thus one of them holds the vendor, another enjoys her upper charms, a third uses her mouth, a fourth makes do with the backside, while the fifth enters her yoni for a "touchdown."

In this way they may go on enjoying her various portals alternately until everyone has scored.

The same things may be done when several Heads of State are sitting in the company of a buxom journalist.

Thus ends the various kinds of congress. There is a most significant sutra on the subject, as follows:

"An ingenious person should multiply the kinds of congress after the beasts and the birds. His knowledge will surely win him the love and respect of every precious yoni."

The Marquis de Sade's Elements of Style

Sade ... {his} pornographic messages are embodied in sentences so pure they might be used as grammatical models.

—Roland Barthes
The Pleasure of the Text

Introduction

Ten days prior to the storming of the Bastille, and long before I had learned to read or write, the Marquis de Sade, France's foremost adult educator and disciplinarian, went on sabbatical to the Charenton lunatic asylum. There, despite inadequate accommodations, he began writing a textbook called *Les Elements du Style*. The manuscript soon became known among the inmate population as *"Cent vingt jours de l'ennui"* – a title prompted less by the author's worthy message than the prose in which he imparted it. Indeed, the work was marred by pedantic repetitions and insufferably bad puns. Such sins might easily have been overlooked had the author chosen to include illustrations.

In 1957, while I was browsing in an adult bookshop on the Champs-Élysées, I stumbled upon the first (and only) edition of *Les éléments du style*, bound in a fellow inmate's flesh. I immediately expressed my disdain at the fact that the slender volume contained not a single picture. The proprietor simply shrugged and spat at my feet. Still, I detected among the book's yellowed pages rich deposits of gold amid the dust and rhetorical debris. It was, I realized, the Marquis de Sade's parvum opus, his attempt to cut the French student body down to size and to instill a sense of badly needed discipline.

What struck me then was the realization that the American academic community could greatly benefit from the master's instructions. I decided to take a crack at the work, to edit it and whip it into shape, so to speak.

In the English classes of today, this "little book" is surrounded by longer, harder, better-endowed tomes. Perhaps it has become something of a curiosity, for even though few students heed its advice, they seem to enjoy reading it. For me, this little book maintains its original stature, standing erect, resolute, and assured. I still find Sade's cruel wisdom a comfort, his rancor a delight, and his penetrating insight into right and wrong, a blessing. His last words linger on:
"Education *smarts.*"

E. B. Whipe

Elementary Rules of Usage

Form the possessive singular of nouns by adding 's.

Follow this rule whatever the final consonant. Thus write,

> Charles's battered paramour
> Lady Burns's lacerations
> the monk's testicles

A common error is to write *it's* for *its*, or vice versa. The first is a contraction, meaning "it is." The second is a possessive.

> It's a wise woman who enjoys having
> her clitoris rubbed by prelates and her
> vagina sucked by barons.

> Its intrusion in life seemed a lesson in
> buggery.

In a series of three or more terms with a single conjunction, use a comma after each term except the last.

Thus write,

> young girls enticed into a life of debauchery,
> children abandoned, wives humiliated, and
> several suicides

Do not break sentences in two.

In other words, do not use periods for commas.

> A whore is a charming creature. Young.
> Voluptuous. Who sacrifices her reputation
> for the happiness of others.

Enclose pathetic expressions between brackets.

> [Tenderness, trust, the nicest restraint and
> the most severe modesty crowned his mar-
> riage.] In making himself the happiest of
> men he was clever enough to make the most
> libertine of girls his mistress.

This rule is difficult to apply, for it is frequently hard to
decide whether a brief phrase is, in fact, pathetic.

Whip dull paragraphs into shape.

> And so the marquis departed. His journey was
> short, and he returned two days later. He was
> feeling ill and went straight to bed.

The above passage is pedestrian at best. Compare it with
the following:

> And so the marquis departed. His journey was
> short, and he returned two days later, escorted
> by two policemen, and furnished with an

alleged order, the mere sight of which caused the president to tremble in every limb.

Elementary Principles of Composition

Omit needless words.

Madame de Gernande, aged nineteen, had the most lovely, the most noble, the most majestic figure one could hope to see. Not one of her gestures, not a single movement was without gracefulness, not one of her glances lacked depth of sentiment, nothing could equal the expression of her eyes, which were a beautiful dark brown, although her hair was blond; but a certain languor, a lassitude entailed by her misfortunes, dimmed their eclat, and thereby rendered them a thousand times more interesting; her skin was very fair, her hair very rich; her mouth was very small, perhaps too small, and I was little surprised to find this defect in her: 'twas a pretty rose not yet in full bloom; but teeth so white ... lips of a vermilion ... one might have said Love had colored them with tints borrowed from the goddess of flowers; her nose was aquiline, straight, delicately modeled; upon her brow curved two ebony eyebrows; a perfectly lovely chin; a visage, in one word, of the finest oval shape over whose entirety reigned a kind of attractiveness, a naivete, an openness which might well have made one take this adorable face for an angelic rather than mortal physiognomy. Her arms, her breasts, her flanks were of a splendor ... of a round fullness fit to serve as models to an artist; a black silken fleece covered her mons veneris, which was sustained by two superbly cast thighs; and what astonished me was that, despite the slenderness of the Countess's figure, despite her sufferings, nothing had impaired the firm quality of her flesh: her round, plump buttocks were as smooth, as ripe, as firm as if her figure were heavier and as if she had always dwelled in the depths of happiness. However, frightful traces of her husband's libertinage were scattered thickly about; but, I repeat, nothing spoiled, nothing damaged ... the very image of a beautiful lily upon which the honeybee has inflicted some scratches. To so many gifts Madame de Gernande added a gentle nature, a romantic and tender mind, a heart of such sensibility!

The paragraph above may be reduced to the following sentence:

Madame de Gernande was a piece of ass.

Avoid a succession of loose sentences.

Make an unbreakable habit of daintiness. Always start the day with clean underwear and hosiery. If you haven't time or strength to iron crepe slips and panties, wear the knit variety that needs no pressing. But don't get an "extra day's wear" from your lingerie. There is little difference between *dirty* underwear and *slightly soiled* underwear.

Apart from its triteness and emptiness, the paragraph above is bad because of the structure of its sentences, with their mechanical symmetry and singsong. Compare these sentences:

"Wait one moment," says the berserk monk. "I want to flog simultaneously the most beautiful of behinds and the softest of breasts." He leaves me on my knees and, bringing Armande toward me, makes her stand facing me with her legs spread, in such a way that my mouth touches her womb and my breasts are exposed between her thighs and below her behind; by this means the monk has what he wants before him: Armande's buttocks and my titties in close proximity: furiously he beats them both, but my companion, in order to spare me blows which are becoming far more dangerous for me than for her, has the goodness to lower herself and thus shield me by receiving upon her own person the lashes that would inevitably have wounded me.

Use definitive, specific, concrete language.

These groupings were frequent; for when a monk indulged in whatever form of pleasure, all the girls regularly surrounded him in order to fire all his parts' sensations, that voluptuousness might, if one may be forgiven the expression, more surely penetrate into him through every pore.

Place the emphatic words of a sentence at the end.

The proper place in the sentence for the word or group of words that the writer desires to make most prominent is usually the end.

... You, Eugénie, bestow two good smacks upon Madame your Mother, and as soon as she gains the threshold, help her cross it with a few lusty kicks aimed at her ass.

A Few Matters of Form

Numerals. Do not spell out dates or other serial numbers. Write them in figures or in Roman notation, as may be appropriate.

October 29 — By order of the King, the Marquis de Sade
is committed to Vincennes fortress for excesses committed in a brothel which he has been frequenting for a month.

Les 120 journées de Sodome ou l'école du libertinage

1. As regards the laws of Nature only, is this act really criminal?

Quotations. When a quotation is followed by an attributive phrase, the comma is enclosed within the quotation marks.

"On your knees," the monk said to me. "I am going to whip your titties."

Titles.

> *Les journées de Florbelle, ou la Nature dévoilée,
> suivies des mémoires de l'abbé de Modose et des
> aventures d'Emilie de Voinange servant de preuves
> aux assertions, ouvrage orné de deux cents gravures.*

For the titles of literary works, a good rule of thumb is: a title should never exceed the length of the author's penis.

Colloquialisms. If you use a colloquialism or a slang word or phrase, simply use it; do not draw attention to it by enclosing it in quotation marks.

> "I'm not that kind of girl."

Exclamations. Do not attempt to emphasize simple statements by using a mark of exclamation.

> I engaged fifteen men, alone; in twenty-four hours,
> I was ninety times fucked!

The exclamation mark is to be reserved for use after true exclamations or commands.

> — Oh, please, dear friend, allow me to frig
> this splendid member!

> "Oh, Great God!" I exclaimed, casting myself
> at Roland.

Words and Expressions Commonly Misused

Enormity. Use only in the sense of "monstrous wickedness." Misleading, if not wrong, when used to express bigness.

virtuous. Might mean "objectionable," "disconcerting," "distasteful." Select instead a word whose meaning is clear: "frigid."

to lick into shape. Use it sparingly. Save it for specific application.

finishing school. Often unnecessary.

split infinitive. There is precedent from the fourteenth century down for interposing an adverb between to and the infinitive it governs, but the construction should be avoided unless the writer wishes to place unusual stress on the adverb.

to diligently *whip*   to *whip* diligently

to flog a dead horse. Means one thing when applied to men, another when applied to horses.

bugger. Often used because to the writer it sounds more impressive than "bumming." Such usage is not incorrect but is to be guarded against.

An Approach to Style (with a List of Reminders)

Write in a way that comes naturally.

Write in a way that comes easily and naturally to you, using phrases that come readily to hand.

> "And now spread them, Madame," the Count said brutally.

Do not affect a breezy manner.

The volume of writing is enormous these days, and much of it has a sort of windiness about it, almost as though the author were in a state of euphoria.

> The impure monk uninterruptedly occupied with me in like fashion, then told me to give the largest possible vent to whatever winds might be hovering in my bowels, and these I was to direct into his mouth.

The breezy style is often the work of an egocentric, the person who imagines that everything that pops into his head is of general interest.

Make sure the reader knows who is speaking.

Dialogue is a total loss unless you indicate who the speaker is. In long dialogue passages containing no attributives, the reader may become lost and be compelled to go back and reread in order to puzzle the thing out.

> "But the man you describe is a monster."
> "The man I describe is in tune with Nature."
> "He is a savage beast."
> "'Tis impossible."
> "Impossible?"
> "Absolutely."
> "Could you explain?"
> "No, that's our secret."

Avoid fancy words.

Avoid the elaborate, the pretentious, the coy and the cute. Do not be tempted by a twenty-dollar word when there is a ten-center handy, ready and able.

> asphyxiation
> Stockholm syndrome
> victimological
> *crime passionel*
> guillotine
> pornokitsch
> assault and battery
> poetic punishment

bludgeon
garrote
sadomasochist
post mortem

Be clear.

In the very thick or disorder and corruption,
all of what mankind calls happiness may shed
itself bountifully upon life; not let this cruel
and fatal truth cause no alarm; let honest folk
be no more seriously tormented by the example
we are going to present of disaster everywhere
dogging the heels of virtue; this criminal felicity
is deceiving, it is seeming only; independently
of the punishment most certainly reserved by
Providence for those whom success in
crime has seduced, do they not nourish in the
depths of their soul a worm which unceasingly
gnaws, prevents them from finding joy in these
fictive gleams of meretricious well-being, and
instead of delights, leaves naught in their soul
but the rending memory of the crimes which
have led them to where they are?

Clarity, clarity, clarity. When you become hopelessly mired
in a sentence, it is best to start fresh:

To these horrors Madame de Lorsange added three
or four infanticides.

Avoid the use of qualifiers.

Rather, very, little, pretty – these are the leeches that infest the pond of prose, sucking the blood of words.

> Upon the first day of every month each monk adopts a girl who must serve a term as his servant and as the target of his very shameful desires.

Use a dash to set off an abrupt break or interruption.

> "Thérèse," he says, "you are going to suffer cruelly" — he had no need to tell me so, for his eyes declared it.

Prefer the standard to the offbeat.

The young writer will be drawn at every turn toward eccentricities in language. He will hear the heat of new vocabularies, the exciting rhythms.

> A third girl, kneeling before him, begins to excite him with her hands, and a fourth, completely naked, indicates with her fingers where he must strike my body. Gradually, this girl begins to arouse me, and what she does to me Antonin does as well, with both his hands, to two other girls on his left and right.

Use orthodox spelling.

In ordinary composition, use orthodox spelling. Do not write *Mame* for *maim*.

Do not explain too much.

Two nights later, I slept with Jérome; I will not describe his horrors to you; they were still more terrifying.

It is seldom advisable to tell all.

INDEX

François de Sade

The Wonderful Wizard of Sade

or Well Chastised in Kansas

O thou my friend!
The prosperity of Crime is like unto the lightning
whose traitorous brilliancies
sabotage the atmosphere but for an instant
in order to hurl into death's very depths
the luckless one they have dazzled.

ACT I. The Cyclone

Dorothy — an All-American girl with a virginal air, large blue eyes very soulful and appealing, a dazzling fair skin, a supple and resilient body, a touching voice (oh, how she could sing!), teeth of ivory, and the loveliest blond hair — lived in the midst of the great Kansas prairies.

She shared a modest home with her Uncle Henry, a debaucherous farmer and his voluptuous wife, Auntie Em, who was known around town as "the slut." The term was not a pejorative, mind you, but was spoken with great affection. After all, the town's population was only 38 and largely male.

At this period crucial to the virtue of the maiden, Dorothy was in one day made bereft of nearly everything: a frightful cyclone precipitated her family into circumstances so cruel it is nearly impossible to describe them. Indeed, the images haunt one like a ghostly reflection glimpsed in a recurring nightmare.

Yet, failure to describe the horrors that occurred would leave us bereft of narrative, with nothing but a shopworn anecdote such as the one about the traveling salesman.

One wintry night during a typical Kansas blizzard, a traveling salesman's car became stuck in a snowbank. It took the young man several hours to make his way on foot through bitter winds to the nearest farm house. Frozen half to death, he trudged up to the front door and knocked.

After what seemed like an eternity, a grizzled old farmer opened the door and eyed the shivering stranger with suspicion. "Whatcha doing on my property?"

"My car broke down and I need a place to spend the night," pleaded the salesman.

The farmer scratched at his beard, then nodded. "Sure, young fella, I can give ya a place to bunk, but I ain't got no daughter for you to sleep with, like ya always hear about in them thar jokes."

The salesman brushed some ice off his jacket, thought for a moment and asked: "How far is it to the next farm?"

* * *

Meanwhile, back at the farm, the small, ramshackle structure was lifted like a leaf above the earth and carried to a strange land where it was deposited with such ferocity that it was reduced to a heap of lumber. The decapitated corpses of its owners — Uncle Henry and Aunt Em — lay beside the couple's four-poster bed which — surprisingly — remained unscathed.

Oddly enough, the horrid cyclone had spared Dorothy and her little dog, Toto, leaving them gently on the bed in the midst of a landscape of marvelous beauty. There were lovely patches of greensward all about, and tall, erect trees bearing rich and luscious fruits. Banks of colorful flowers sprang forth, and birds with rare and brilliant plumage soared and sang.

Dorothy climbed down to confront her new surroundings. As she stood all atremble, gawking at the strange and beautiful sights, she noticed a group of mini-monks advancing toward her. Their robes were raised to reveal their nakedness and — although not as big as grown men — sexual organs of gigantic proportions! Indeed, they were having great difficulty maintaining their equilibrium as they marched – intermittently pitching forward, propelled by the weight of their grotesque phalluses.

One old monk finally sauntered up to Dorothy and attempted to bow. His glans struck the ground with a great *thummmp* – then bounced back and struck him in the forehead. He winced and groaned, yet regained his dignity. "*You*, young lady, are *not* welcome in the land of the Munchkin Monks!" he proclaimed. Brutality, libertinage — all the characteristics of the debauchee — glittered in his cunning stare.

"Look — you've killed the Wicked Bitch of the East, our faithful Mistress! You've freed us from our bondage!"

"*You fool!*" cried another Munchkin libertine, waving his organ like a sword. "See what you've done!"

"Take off your clothes!" demanded the cantankerous monk.

"Strip naked?!" exclaimed Dorothy. "Oh, Heavens!"

The old debauchee's flames of passion erupted with violence as a stroke of lightning. He proceeded to disrobe the poor girl in furious fashion, while a second monk forced her to kneel between his legs. A third came forth and slapped her bare backside, powerfully but in a very nervous manner, attacking her cheeks and breasts. Another impure dwarf descended and began to suckle and bite her big toe.

Dorothy blushed, her chest turned red, her toe purple. She implored the munching Munchkins to spare her these humiliations. Tears leapt from her eyes like sailors abandoning ship. Her weeping served only to accelerate their monk-lust; they fondled, poked, bit, banged, smacked, whacked, thrashed and lashed.

Toto darted over, leapt in the air, and bit Dorothy in the armpit. "*Stop it, you imbecile! Bite my tormentors!*"

"Yes!" cried the littlest monk, who waddled forward, dragging his tumescent staff along the ground. He turned his back and squatted, offering up his buttocks to the mutt. "Bite me!"

Toto commenced to sniff the midget's posterior, then

scampered off into the bushes and peed.

Looking chagrined, Dorothy turned to the old monk. "Defile my dog," she snapped.

ACT II. The City of Golden Showers

"Where are you going?" asked the Sinful Tinman.

"We are on our way to the City of Golden Showers to see the Great Sade," Dorothy answered. "I want him to send me back to Kansas, and the Scarecrow..." she blushed, "...he, uh, wants to be whipped upon his bare buttocks."

'Hmmm...' The Sinful Tinman appeared to think deeply for a moment. Then he said: "Do you suppose the powerful Sade might spend some seed upon this rusty tin body?"

"Um . . . I . . . I guess so," stammered the girl. "I have no experience in such things, although I've heard it said that it's a perversion. You seem to desire something that grievously offends Nature."

"What charming innocence, my dear, what childishness," retorted the Sinful Tinman.

'The wasting of the seed destined to perpetuate the human species, dear girl, is the only crime which can exist. Such is the hypothesis; according to it, seed is put in us for the sole purpose of reproduction, and if that were true I would grant you that diverting it is an offence. But once it is demonstrated that by situating this semen in men's loins is by no means enough to warrant supposing that Nature's purpose is to have all of it employed for reproduction, what then does it matter, Dorothy, whether it be spilled in one place or another?"

"I never thought of it like that before," admitted the girl.

ACT III. Home Again

Determined to have the last word and, indeed, imbued with the power to do so, the author — Donatien Alphonse François, Marquis de Sade — appeared on the page. In his hands he held all that remained of his virtuous heroine – a small, bleached skull. As if meditating in preparation for a soliloquy, he fixed his gleaming gaze upon the sorry specimen. Then, extending it high above his head, as if offering an exhibition to the heavens and, with uncharacteristic concision, proclaimed the following epigram:

"Yes, dear Dorothy," said the Marquis to the skull, "there's no face like bone."

Closet Sade

With the recent discovery of an unpublished manuscript by the Marquis de Sade (1740-1814), it can now be revealed that the infamous French writer was in fact a disturbed 'fabric-hater.' This obscure text entitled La philosophie dans l'armoire, *was considered too shocking even by its author and was abandoned in mid- seam. The following excerpt is complete and unexpurgated.*

Meanwhile, Rodin, greatly aroused, had seized the girl's pink peignoir, tied it to a post in the middle of the closet. Rodin dwells upon the innocent dressing gown, is fired by it, and dares to bite its hem. Now able to proceed without restraint, he removes his zoot suit and commences to assault the other helpless garments which tremble upon their hangers like trapped bass upon hooks. What gowns! What pyjamas! What culottes! And who is this monster that seeks pleasure in the defilement of fabric? Rodin contemplates his victims ... his inflamed eye roves from silk to khaki, his hands dare pinch a petrified poncho, profane a pinafore, humiliate a halter. Now the libertine tears a tunic with his teeth, rips the buttons from a trench coat, fondles a frock and shamelessly wrinkles a kimono. His mounting wrath exceeds all limits as he savages a brand-new sweater and tortures a tuxedo. Presently he resorts to cruel invectives, damning designer jeans to hell, lambasting bustles and besmirching Bermudas, proclaiming the sins of T-shirts and G-strings. He wrestles with a windbreaker and crumples a cardigan. He destroys a red dickey and slaps a pair of purple slacks. He snatches up an alligator belt that has been soaking in a vat of vinegar to give it tartness and sting.

"Well now," says he, at last approaching the virgin peignoir, "prepare yourself, you have got to suffer; he swings a vigorous arm and the belt is brought down upon the cloth: twenty-five strokes are applied: the tender pink rosiness of this matchless material is in a thrice torn to shreds, while poor Julie emits cries which echo off the mothballs and fill my soul with despair. There is nothing I can do to save her garment from this fate.

Up Fanny Hill

A Run-on Sentence by a Woman of Pleasure

Being composed of the First Few Words from Each of the Original Volume's 600 Paragraphs & Forming, in a Single Sentence, an Expurgated Version of the Text by John Cleland.

Madam, I sit hating truth, stark, naked this, and my father, my education, my poor mother, I was now entering on as I had now nobody nor can I remember, the idea however of having places, then, being taken, she took indeed great care, it was pretty but guess at my mortification instead, then, whilst I stood thus stupid left thus alone, one of the waiters coming, 'tis incredible what accordingly, I made up then to Madam having heard me out on this, I drew back presently, assuming she look'd, yes, and please upon this Madam was, however, this being over, you may be sure, here my mistress first, presently, my mistress touch'd Martha, who was in the midst of here, dinner was now at table, it was here, no sooner then was this encouraged by this, her hands, the flattering praises, I lay then all tame and my breasts, if but not contented instead of which, in the meantime, for my part, I was Phoebe, herself, the hackney'd, no, says Phoebe, you must, after a sufficient length, in the morning we breakfasted, imagine to yourself, Madam, the care of dressing, and Phoebe's tall, yet not well dress'd, I was after some, imagine to yourself a man, this then was the monster, however, I was Phoebe, however, Mother Brown was at dinner, Mrs. Brown and thus they sat down fronting me, and tea over, we were now alone, but long the brute had, it seems, when it was over he yet, whilst this confusion of ideas, after some pause, he ask'd as much, however, as soon such, too, and so I pass'd then the time, about eleven at night, Mrs. Brown withdrawn, Phoebe the youth is soon raised, and Mrs. Brown, who had touched accordingly, they were let in conversation, example, all, in short, I was soon pretty well, in the mean time, preachments of morality hitherto, I instantly crept softly, and oh! how still and hush I had not much droll was it to see her paramour sat down as he stood, but I soon had her sturdy stallion long, however, the young spark prepared then, and disposed whilst they were in, after which, my senses recover'd, the young fellow had my pious governess, however, I admired this, over they both went out as soon as I heard the opportunity, however, Phoebe could not hear it but, on her sounding Phoebe on this, she asked me, you may at five in the evening, we went down the back-stairs, the young gentleman after saluting her, presently, as if this had been when he saw this, this girl could not be the young Italian, still, in the meantime, the young gentleman, by Phoebe, at this, by this time when he had finished his, for my part, here was no room either, we had certainly the young foreigner but who could count, in the meantime, but guess my surprise when for me Phoebe lay down, I opened the parlour door, but when I drew nearer, figure to yourself, but on seeing his shirt-collar it seems that I told him then, never, however, for besides our little plan was that I then just hinted the risks to this purpose were the fluctuations of my mind, I got to the street-door, my eyes were instantly fill'd in an instant, for an old jolly stager, who I wish'd after breakfast, whilst Charles had my bosom in the meantime, I being now too

high, I complain'd but he tries again, still Charles alas, he
now resumes his attempts, when I recover'd my senses, the
sore was, however, after dinner, and as he is now in bed,
yes, even at this time, nor was it till after how often when
thus we lay together that night, late in the morning, it was
then broad day oh! could the parting, then the platform,
nor did his shirt hinder his thighs, finely fashioned, but I
lay down then, and I, struggling faintly, could not but now,
this visit, in our calmer intervals, Charles was, however, as
after dinner, which we ate accordingly, on being let in, the
Madam was immediately sent down, it is peculiar to
Phoebe, this negotiation had, however, taken long, however,
I was still a-bed, yet I could not help laughing, we supped
with all, he came to bed thus, making the most of Charles,
he arrived at our new lodgings, the landlady, Mrs. Jones, a
sketch of her, she was about forty-six, when she saw such
in this hopeful sanctuary, and here, however, under the
wings, as to the men I saw my love in our cessations, I was
in my country, as to money, though, our landlady, Mrs.
Jones, but the barbarity of two life-long days, far she had
not, the maid readily came, in consequence of which thus
was the idol of the maid when Mrs. Jones return'd, she had
hardly fmish'd the cruel, thus I lay six weeks time, however,
the landlady had all, she told me, Mrs. Jones however,
judging in this situation, the gentleman, on his entering,
the tea was made, at this so delicate and whilst he was
exposing to all his speeches, the sight, however, still the
gentleman, however, no violent passions had, he was,
however, so regardful as the evening was, presently, a neat
and elegant supper, the maid quitting at supper, after I had
now got there, Mr. H. who had, accordingly, the maid, as
she had hardly time, the bed shook again, I had it now, I

felt yet oh! what an immense Mr. H ... Mr. H ... , he was about eleven, in came Mrs. Jones, but as soon as he was gone, yet, he did not return till we soon got to the house, he stayed the morning, I was now establish'd, Mr. H. as Mr. B .... so experienc'd, he made suppers, we visited, but I had now the first sight that had I lov'd the least delicate of all, as for the wench, had I considered this, nor was this Mr. H., in order when I saw him, when I thought I was then lying, I bid him come towards I, smiling, my lips, which I threw, but what was yet but it was now by my direction, however, but I expected then, but when I made him easily, novelty, I was now so bruised, giddy and intoxicated whilst in the close of the next morning, waking, struck with this apprehension, but the silky hair, this continuation of finding then every thing, all dispositions, 1 could not but observe his hair, and why should I here suppress Mr. H.'s loftier qualifications, we may say, with this he advanced, then I smiled, and here began the usual, when I slipping, and here, Madam, as love never had my happiness, however, I gave a great scream, as confused as I was, in the meantime, presently, without adding to the guilt, Mr. H., Madam, then, for you, at these words, he went, and I was now as though I should have been, as in the meantime, but this, the fifty guineas promis'd my maid, I had discharged, we soon got to my lodgings, I was now, Madam, if I imagined, what you say resuming though here, in the outer parlour, to the sameness of our sex, as soon after having after dinner, Mrs. Cole, embark'd as I was, this point thus adjusted amidst all but Mrs. Cole, I thought, my governess, after her name, neither my extraction, as night drew on before either of us undressed, but the pleasure in the order of my father was neither better, the family had not been there, my first emotions, this time, but how quick it seems here, Louisa, the brunette whom, according to practical maxims, I now shunn'd, but these, but frequency of man alone, I almost, what shall I say?, this affair had, however, here Louisa, Mrs. Cole on the landingplace, on my entrance, aw'd and confounded, they assur'd me that in the midst, as soon as my countenance expressed no doubt, I the first, by this time the second, and, surely, never did Harriet, her lover, her legs, her truly enamor'd gallant, who, as soon as he was off, and now Emily's partner, had taken her gallant, as soon as the frolick was to Mrs. Cole, by the way, I now stood before my friend, but now the company, as it was she, here I stayed with this noble and this event also, but I had now pass'd whilst I was chaffering, for as soon then the next morning, the girls all, and effectively, in concluding, she went, regardful, however, thus she led him when the night then was fix'd, everything then being disposed, as meanwhile, at scarce thirty, he had, as soon in each case now, and you would ask me perhaps, recover'd you may guess how, leaving, I was now restor'd, in the meantime, Mr. Norbert, who, sometimes, one evening when this was over, but I had now his sister, Lady L, for whom Mrs. Cole, this Mrs. Cole, my good temporal mother, was, I stood, I was then as Mr. Barville saw, but whilst he was exceedingly fair, as after next we took from stooping, I led him, seizing, I was resuming then the rod, then my gentleman here he thank'd me, consonant to this disposition, he had all my back parts, you may guess, as soon as I sat down, but Mr. Barville, no stranger, I had now achiev'd this, I was not, however, Mrs. Cole, to whom this was another peculiarity, you may be sure, Louisa, this I had here, whilst I was a spirit of curiosity, the eldest, the youngest, but after a look for now, in the rashness then of the criminal scene, when I came home again, but one morning the boys and servants, this boy, Louisa, as we went up, consequently, I, for my part, who had Louisa, Louisa then stopped by the bed, poor Louisa, gorg'd, Louisa lay pleas'd, as for whether she ever return'd, Louisa herself did not, but everything being settled, after tea, Emily, who never refus'd anything, then, as here I wav'd and wanton'd, there, thus Emily, who meanwhile, in a time, for accordingly we at the same time resuming now my history, this too was Emily's last, but it was not so easy, these desertions, thus I had here, under the new character, I was scarce, however, he was, as but referring himself in short, with this gentleman, after acquitting myself, I saw myself then, but alas!, given him up I had, as you cannot conceive, I had taken nobody, this had recover'd the first object, all these interjections thus absorbed, the landlady leaving us again, he was there in the interval, Charles, in the meantime, we four then supp'd after the cloth and here, as soon then but now as I kept hesitating, meanwhile, two candles lighted, but as action I have, I believe, somewhere, Charles, I had now totally taken as we were giving them, thus happy, Charles, whose whole frame was but all this pleasure tending but still there (he remembers the journey), Charles and I were here, on the road, but when I opened the plea of love, thus, at length, you laugh, perhaps, if you do then you know Mr. C*** O***, I shall see you soon, Madam, yours, etc.

THE END

Madame Bovary's Training Bra

A Suppressed Episode

We were in class when the head-master came in, followed by a new training bra, not wearing the school uniform, and a school servant carrying a large bandage. Those who had been asleep woke up, and everyone rose as if just surprised at his work.

The head-master made a sign to us to sit down. Then, turning to the class-master, he said in a low tone:

"Monsieur Roger, here is a new brassiere which I recommend to your care." He cleared his throat. "If her, uh, conduct, is satisfactory, she will go to work for Madame Bovary."

The training bra, standing in the corner behind the bed so that she could hardly be seen, was about fifteen and taller than any of us. She feigned a vague, voluptuous air, yet seemed very ill at ease. Although she was not experienced in the ways of undergarments, her attitude was decidedly seductive.

We began repeating our lesson. She listened with all her ears, as attentive as if at a sermon on the sins of lingerie, or perhaps eavesdropping on the adventures of a promiscuous peignoir, not daring even to uncross her legs; and when the alarm bell rang, the master was obliged to tell her to fall into line with the rest of us.

When we came back from the trampoline, we were in the habit of throwing our cups onto the bed so that together they made an overpowering stench; it was the thing, you know, the rage, so to speak. But, whether she had not noticed the trick, or did not dare to attempt it, the training bra was still clutching her tiny cups on her knees even after prayers were over.

"Rise," said the master.

She stood up, dropping her cups.

The whole class began to titter. Blushing, she stooped to pick them up. A neighbor knocked them down again ... she picked them up once more. You can ignore this sentence for it serves no useful purpose. The debacle continued for several minutes.

"Get rid of your cups," ordered the master, who was a bit of a wag, if you catch my drift.

There was a burst of laughter (tittering turned torrential) from the jocks, which so thoroughly put the poor little bra out of countenance that she did not know whether to keep her cups in her hand, leave them on the floor, or put them on her head.

She sat down again and placed them on her knees.

"Rise," repeated the master, "and tell me the name of your manufacturer."

The young brassiere articulated in a stammering voice an unintelligible name. Something like *nghdfdgdyyer.*

"Again, you silly slut!"

The same sputtering of syllables was heard, drowned by the chortles and guffaws, or rather the guffaws and chortles, that issued from the gleeful athletic supporters, myself included.

"Louder!" cried the master. "Louder! Louder!"

The trembling training bra then took a supreme resolution, opened an inordinately large mouth, and shouted at the top of her voice the word "*Maidenform.*" A hubbub broke out, as hubbubs often do, rose in crescendo with bursts of shrill voices (they yelled, barked, stamped, repeated *"Maidenform! Maidenform!..."*), then died away into single notes, growing quieter only with great difficulty, and now and again suddenly recommencing here and there like stifled farts let loose.

However, amid the rain of impositions (feel free to grab a sandwich), order was gradually reestablished in the class (please come back, it's getting good again); and the master having succeeded in catching the name *"Maidenform,"* having had it dictated to him, spelt out, half-anagramed, etc., at once ordered the poor bra to go and sit in the punishment chair at the foot of the master's bed. (See, I told you it was getting good.) He got up to leave, but before going hesitated ...

"What are you looking for now?" asked the master.

"My ... my c-u-p-s," said the training bra, timidly, casting troubled, nymphetic glances at the mob of grinning jocks which now surrounded her.

The master shook his head in exasperation. Madame Bovary would be terribly disappointed in this episode.

"Not too rough, fellows," cautioned the master on his way out the door. "Remember, she has a reputation to uphold!"

My Secret Life with Father

by Anonymous & Clarence Day

One evening when Father and Mother and I were in the library talking, Miss Bassett, a trained whore, came in. She stripped, and in doing that, her movements were graceful and I found her beautiful in form, with thighs which were a perfect model, and a large, though not overpowering backside.

"What makes ladies smell so nice?" said I to Mother.

She turned — as she always did when she was in trouble — to Father.

"Clare," she said urgently, "what makes ladies smell so nice?"

Father scowled. "I don't know, Vinnie, the bum-hole, I suppose."

He had just passed his seventieth birthday and many of his old friends had their pricks into women's arseholes. What angered Father about it was that it seemed to kill healthy men — men who he felt sure would last for the next 20 years.

Miss Bassett stood there waiting for something to happen. I pinched her and said: "I want to frig you — I'll give you five shillings!"

Mother laughed. Father scowled. My prick stiffened.

I looked at Mother. "Please?"

Mother turned to Father and said: "Clare, it's only for one night."

"I don't give a damn, Vinnie. It's dangerous."

"Yes, but Clare," Mother impatiently cried, "Clarence is healthy. Besides, what difference does it make to you?"

The ice was broken. I took off my trousers.

"Oh, well, pshaw," said Father, scowling at me, "if it will satisfy your whim, go ahead."

"Thank you, Father."

Mother laughed uneasily. Father scowled again. Miss Bassett, red-faced and nipples all atwitch, looked at my prick.

"Isn't it a whopper!" she cried.

"Poppycock," said Father, still scowling.

"You ought to be so blessed, Mr. Day," Miss Bassett told him.

Mother tried to reassure him: "I suppose some men have smaller things than yours, Clare."

Father's face slightly stiffened. He rose with concern, walked away, grew quite angry, and said: "Damn it, Vinnie — a lot of them have!"

Meanwhile, I humped Miss Bassett's splendid cunt.

Afterwards, when my joystick had spent itself most fervidly, Mother asked Father if he might ever frig her. They had been married for almost 30 years.

"Pah! Never!" shouted Father.

Mother looked at him, startled but admiring, and whispered to me, "I almost believe he could do it."

A Man and a Maid with Flowers

I think I shall retire for the night,' said Lady Prudwick severely.

From behind a copy of the *Daily Hypocrite* her husband smiled cautiously, having awaited those very words for the better part of the evening. His feigned interest in current events concealed a maze of impure thoughts regarding Wilty Flosil, the downstairs maid, whose abundant charms played havoc with his moral fibre. Now, lowering the tabloid to his chin, Lord Prudwick safely faced his wife.

"Very well, my dear."

Without question, Elmereta Prudwick was the homeliest of women; possessed of a visage that might frighten a hyena. Her figure, alas, was an ill-favored heirloom best kept in the attic under a sheet. Lord Prudwick could not for the life of him recall why he had married her. Something to do with an escrow account. Certainly she had never been seductive, nor the slightest bit flirtatious. No indeed. She was a rampart – a fortress to be defended at all costs from unknown forces which conspired to storm her dreary fortifications.

"Coming up, Llewellyn?"

Her voice a burst of cannon fire across the quiet study. The smoke of her suspicion rising black to haunt the air.

"In a bit," replied Lord Prudwick, affecting an attitude of exaggerated nonchalance. "I'll just finish this, uh, rather extraordinary report ..." He searched the page for a suitable distraction. "Yes, here it is, the death of Percy Hunkford—

have you heard? Grisly business, I daresay. Took his own life with a scythe. Quite messy, listen to this — "

"Llewellyn! You insensitive *boor*."

"How silly of me, of course."

"Of course, and quite *typical*. Thinking nothing of my gentle nature. Well I shan't waste my breath at this hour. I'll expect a full apology at breakfast. Good *night*!"

"Good night, dear."

Bloody pompous baboon ...

Lord Prudwick glanced at the clock on the mantelpiece. Despite the late hour he remained in his chair, counting the minutes whilst his wife, upstairs, prepared her toilet. After a sufficient interval he rose and made tracks to the servant's bedchamber.

In no mood for etiquette he dispensed with his usual *tap-tap-tap* on the domestic's door, simply opened it and dashed inside. The room, humble as ever, was shadowed with the scent of sleep, silent but for Wilty's rhythmic breathing — a melodic sound which echoed from her pillow to the patriarch's ear, prompting comparison with his wife's nocturnal outbursts. For despite his separate quarters above, Lord Prudwick was subjected nightly to a cacophonous concert of howls, grunts, snorts and groans, accompanied by guttural sputters and savage gastric blasts. These vile noises, he believed, were part of a plot to drive him mad. Instead, they drove him downstairs.

On her bed, the maid lay dreaming ... of festive balls she would never attend: of her own estate with persons to serve *her*, to bring her tea and tuck her in; of colourful gardens and extravagant gowns. All this in addition to an unpleasant apparition which insinuated itself most rudely: a large phallic-shaped feather-duster that pursued her through dark passageways.

Lord Prudwick eyed the sleeping figure which, divested of quilt, seemed the very essence of servility in nightdress and cap. Presently, his passions aroused, he commenced to disrobe post-haste.

Thus, Wilty Flosil awoke to discover her employer stark naked, throbbing *orchid* in hand, hovering over the bed. "Oh, me goodness," she gasped, taken aback by the sight of the intruder's stiff *petunia*, so heartily hung and pointed directly at her.

"I've come to *dodder* in your *flytrap*," he announced, brandishing his *harebell* like a swollen sword of yore. "Feast your eyes on my mighty *magnolia!*"

For emphasis Lord Prudwick throttled his hot *foxtail*; an action causing the bulbous tip to turn a purplish hue — the grand *gladiolus* fully engorged, straining fervidly with a life all its own.

He proudly waved the prized *goldenrod* and shouted: "No pansy's *peony* this, eh?"

Wilty Flosil was compelled to admit, albeit privately, that her employer's *cudweed* was the biggest in the county; however, temptation was tempered by fear.

"Please, sir, leave me be ... it's frightfully late and I've got me chores so early —"

"To hell with the bloody chores, I'm *hornbeam!*"

'If only he'd *jonquil* and be done with it,' thought Wilty rather hopelessly, as she knew full well that he was not about to settle for self-abuse.

Indeed, Lord Prudwick climbed on to the bed and ordered her to turn over so that he might *fuschia* from behind.

"Hurry up, you blooming *wisteria!*"

"I beg you, sir, not in me *azalea* ... it still be sore from last time. In me *vanilla* if you must."

Pulling off her nightdress, Lord Prudwick embraced the maid lecherously and lavished lewd kisses on her bountiful white *begonias*. His *thistle* darted deftly at her stiff little *nosegays*, dancing round the big, pink *auriculas*, lapping rapturously the *knickis* as they jiggled.

These urgent attentions rapidly reduced the domestic to quivers, until she fairly swooned in his *fronds*. Free at last from the chains of propriety, she was a pliant *darnel* in the *dandelion's* den!

While his *tulips* continued their *honeysuckle* of her voluptuous *buttercups*, Prudwick's hands grew bolder. His fingers found her firm bare *burdocks*, encircling each *buglo* and brazenly squeezing her *hops*, as she squirmed to avoid his pinky which sought entrance at her *asphodel*. This defensive manoeuvre was met with force: Lord Prudwick administering a sharp spanking to her *bunchberries*.

"Take, that, you little *whorl!*"

Beneath the blows her *aster* flushed crimson, the *moonwort* full and bright.

"Don't stop," moaned Wilty, her *mallows* atremble, as dutifully she explored her master's patch of *furze*; running her hands through the forest of *gorse*, down to where his *tansies* dangled in their hairy *privet* — the bilberries big as Prince Albert's *kingcups!* She gently tweaked them with one hand, as the other pruned the roots of his ribald *gardenia*, weeding about in the *fleur-de-lis* until, suddenly bored, she decided to change course. She ascended the stalwart stem of his *maypop*, tracing with a finger the large blue *vine* which led to the summit. Upon reaching the peak of the *pimpernel*, the maid did measure the circumference in anticipation of what was to come. His hefty *hibiscus*, twitching in the throes of advanced tumescence, posed quite a threat. Would her defenceless *verbena* withstand the onslaught of this strappling *snapdragon*?

"Give me *floral sex!*" cried Lord Prudwick, thrusting his rigid *runnunculus* between her eyes (a slight miscalculation which was promptly corrected). Having abandoned her *buxus blossoms* slick with *salvia*, he devoted himself to her slender *cowslips* in preparation for the final assault on her *forget-me-not*. Together, in the position known as *sixty-vine*, they supped as though the *bouquet* were going out of fashion.

Struggling to avoid premature *orchis*, Prudwick concentrated on the bearded *crepis* until, suddenly, the pert *periwinkle* began to unfold, revealing as it did the shiny pink *quamoclit* moist with dew! His flickering *thistle*-tip tussled with the clinging *clematis*, and poor Wilty was forced to surrender his *petunia* with a loud "*poppy*"!

She could bear it no longer.

"*Fig* me! *Flax* me! Shove your throbbing *crocus* up me *phlox!*"

Now it was her master's turn to play the slave as, with all deliberate speed, Prudwick positioned himself between her outspread *leaves* and introduced his bulging *juniper* into her frothy *chrysanthemum*. In frantic *hemlock* they thrashed upon the flowerbed, at long last joined in joyous *hoyabella*. Wilty's juicy *primrose* lunged to meet his pumping *poinsettia*, the *petal-head* plunging to the hilt, their *geraniums* grinding in a sea of torrid *top-soil!* They rose to the heights of *Jacob's ladder* and beyond, where the mad spasms of *carnation* climaxed as Prudwick's *plumbago* exploded, flooding her fertile *fennel* with a burst of burning *jasmine*!!!

* * *

In her bedroom Lady Prudwick drifted slowly off to sleep. A smile of surprising dimension played upon her lips, while she held in her hand the object of this expression. She had found the perfect lover – indefatigable and responsive to her needs. Furthermore, she was convinced that her husband would never discover her indiscretions and this made her satisfaction complete.

Now, unconsciously, she caressed her passive paramour as if it were of flesh and blood ... not simply an artificial *daffodil*.

Lady Chatterley's Loafer

On a frosty morning in March, Clifford and Connie Trotz went for a walk in the forest of footwear. A stiff breeze whistled through the shoe-trees and scuffed the wing-tipped grass surrounding Loafer's Lane. The well-heeled couple paused in the clearing to watch a bronzed babyshoe play in the mud.

"I'm sorry we can't have a pair of our own," sighed Connie.

Clifford, weighing an idea, decided to put his best foot forward.

"It would almost be a good thing if you had a babyshoe by another loafer," he suggested. "It would be just like our own ... we could teach it to walk, flip-flop and carry on. Don't you think it's worth considering?"

Connie frowned. The babyshoe — *her* baby shoe — was just an "it" to him.

"What about the other loafer?" she asked, walking on thin ice, so to speak.

"Does it matter very much, so long as it holds its tongue. You had that penniless loafer in Germany, Herr Birken-stock, remember? And a few sneakers behind my back. All forgotten now." He eyed her curiously. "You and I are in the same boot. If we continue to think on our feet, we ought to be able to arrange this thing. Besides, the real secret of marriage ain't socks. It's *sole*."

Connie winced.

She did not know if he was right or not.

She tried to put herself in his shoes, unable to father footwear of his own. Sure there had been other loafers – in particular, one well-endowed galosh that had swept her off her feet. But her desire for male loafers was somehow only an excursion from her marriage with Clifford; the habit of intimacy formed by years of sharing the same bedroom slippers. 'But then again,' mused Connie, 'if the shoe fits ...'

"And you really wouldn't mind which loafer's babyshoe I got?" she asked him.

"I trust your instinct of decency and selection. You wouldn't just grab the first loafer to come along, now would you?"

"Of course not," snapped Connie, suddenly fearing the possible consequences of her innate promiscuity. What would she do if she ever got athlete's foot? She would have to tell Clifford and then ...

No, she would never be able to tell him. Instead she would simply run away and hide.

Madeleine's Answer

An Erotic Lipogram

A t well-nigh nineteen, Madeleine was the prettiest girl in the village. And still a virgin — a rare bird indeed in this degenerate age. Men sensed with ease her pristine state. It was evident in her hesitant manner, her verbal restraint. She might as well have been wearing a banner reading: *I've Never Had Sex.* Perhaps inevitable, this being her plight, she was a target wherever she went.

As a gentle stream inspires the bard with its mere passage, Madeleine stirred men's deepest desires when she glided past in a mini-dress. All aimed their gaze at her slender legs, and heartbeats grew rapid. Ladies sighed and whispered. Men whistled, grinned and leered. The timid girl was trapped in a web where all the spiders wanted her. Strangers tailed her in the mall, their minds abrim with the lewdest images, while evil teens gathered at her jeep and waited. Vampires athirst.

She shed her high heels – dashed at exits – ran and hid behind hedges and trees. She zigzagged amid the swarming hands that grabbed at her breasts and patted her behind. Ill with embarrassment and red as a beet, she sat in her jeep and wept. Where was the Divine Being she served with reverent earnestness? Despite her entreaties and terrible tears, He was never there when she needed Him. Then again, Madeleine maintained that He was penalizing her and she deserved it. She had sinned, and His Divine Reprisal was her inebriating shapeliness. Her ripe breasts, her tender thighs – these were the signs that she'd raised her Master's wrath. Therein grew her disadvantage; He had made her a magnet, a tease, a tantalizing prize. A prize that is never awarded.

And what, dear reader, was this girl's grave sin? Well, it seems that when she was little, Madeleine misspelled His name at a spelling bee held in a parish hall. Later, in the eleventh grade, she repeated her misdeed in tests and term papers, and was given a D- in English. Alas, she hadn't learned six essential letters in the alphabet.

At present, whenever she entered her garden apartment in Tarzana, she was assailed anew. She shared her nest with a rather bad seed – her sister Therese. A dissipated lass, Therese made her sister's shelter a veritable pervert's den; replete with libertines and hashish-eaters. Here, gentlemen and ladies behaved as wild animals, engaged in deviant sex whilst viewing X-rated tapes. Married men swapped their wives, and their wives held hands with transvestites. (The latter were wearing Madeleine's panties and bras!) Hippies balled B-girls and B-girls balled their pimps. Sadists whipped their willing slaves with glee. Lesbians, brandishing ersatz male members, beat themselves senseless in a savage ballet. And Therese, brazen and bare-breasted, presided as the menagerie's ring-master.

Madeleine sped past these heartless heathens, sprang at the stairs and leapt three at a time. At least in her bed she'd be spared their bestial indignities. Nevertheless, when she'd made it inside, she still heard them – their relentless ribald patter – the shrill, libidinal, hard-breathing jazz that wailed till dawn. A dirge, it lingered in her ears, lamenting a sad spirit's demise.

Madeleine believed that Therese and her gang were Satan's agents; their aim: brainwash her and steal her maidenhead. A virgin need be slain at the pagan's alter. Her dilemma was plain. In what manner might she thwart them? And then it hit her – a brilliant idea!

"I'll spell His name right and then He'll save me!"

Easier said than attained.

With Bible in hand, she sat in her bed and made several attempts at mastering the alphabet.

She tried and tried and tried again, still the missing letters evaded her. She banged her head against the wall. She spat. She drew a deep breath and – determined as ever – gave it her all: "J .... e .... s .... a — *darnit!*"

Blinded with tears, Madeleine begged Him, demanded He give her the letters. He was treating her as He might an atheist when she was a believer. It wasn't right. Didn't He see the danger she was in?! She sat stranded in her bed, awaiting His answer.

Alas, He was silent.

Still she stared heavenward, her palms pressed tight, till...

Zzzzzzz...

Madeleine slept, and in her deepest sleep she dreamed. A land where happiness reigned eternal and men didn't desire her. It was springtime here in the bright green hills, where rabbis and priests paraded arm in arm, and angels with harps glided in air. And there was Therese ... dressed in wimple and habit, singing His praises. (A dream indeed!) It was all Madeleine wanted, a blessed realm where the Bible was law.

Then, an eerie image appeared; a large, livid steeple

in the distant mist. It grew bigger and bigger, gathering strength, its stem expanding and swelling with veins. It was palpitant... threatening ... *alive*. The angels shed their harps and split. The saints ran hither and thither, alarmed, as the steeple's tip started spewing a strange pale lava!

Massive waves swept the prim villagers with savage speed, swamping their Eden.

"Help!" bawled Madeleine. "I'm a terrible swimmer!"

She was treading lava when Therese — sans habit — sailed past in a pirate's ship.

"Save me, Therese!" pleaded Madeleine, thrashing in the tepid tide.

"I'm late, dear," explained her sister, grinning. She waved at Madeleine and disappeared.

Her strength was diminishing, the end seemed near. Then she heard a man in the mist.

"Relax," he whispered, "it's all a nightmare."

Madeleine realized he wasn't in her dream. She started alert — a stranger was at her bedside! She grabbed the sheet and shielded her breasts.

"Timid, eh?"

"What's the meaning — ??"

" — Sweet Madeleine, I'm mad with desire. Let's get married!"

"*What???*"

He was mad alright, that was plain.

"Married," he repeated. "As in 'wedding bells.'"

"I beg thee, sir, please leave with haste."

The stranger smiled. "We aren't in an Elizabethan drama," he reminded her.

"What nerve!" said she. Still, in her private mind, she admitted he wasn't all that bad. Tall, well-dressed (he even had a tie), and shaven. Perhaps intelligent, albeit ill-mannered.

"Be mine," he said, drawing nearer. "We'll live in a trailer and travel the earth." He lit a pipe. "I hear Tibet is pleasant in the spring."

"Leave! *Right this min* — er, this *instant!*"

His smile widened.

"I mean it," warned Madeleine. "Hasta la vista."

"All right," he sighed, "I get the message." He tapped his pipe in his hand. "Perhaps I was a bit rash. Marriage is a big step and ... well, we've never met." At this, Madeleine gritted her teeth. He stared as she pressed the sheet against her breasts, delineating the salient nipples. A devilish gleam appeared in his irises. "Let's at least have sex."

"BEAT IT!!!"

Her anger served as a philter, whetted his appetite. He grabbed the sheet and drew it aside, revealing her bare gems.

"Even better than I imagined," he sniggered.

"Rape!" wailed Madeleine, as she tried retrieving the sheet. She wrestled with him, bit his hand, and still he retained it. "Rape!"

"It'll be legal when we're married."

She sighed, resigned. The battle had tired her, sapped her spirit. He sat beside her and she went limp in his arms. He held her tight.

"I passed the AIDS test," he bragged. "Besides, I earn a great deal. I'm a TV star."

'$$$$ ...' she meditated. Then, having weighed this detail in her mind, she brightened. There were advantages, she realized, in being a bride; even when the nitwit wasn't Mr. Right.

"Shall we wed then?" said the stranger, handing her an emerald ring.

"What the hell," said Madeleine.

Later that evening, she traded in her title "Miss" and, at present, was a "Mrs." Mrs. what? She hadn't an idea, as her mate insisted that he remain nameless.

"Give me a hint," said Madeleine.

"Mr. Ed," he teased.

"Ah, well," she sighed, "it isn't essential. Besides, I'm terrible with names." She glared at the heavens and sneered.

When, at last, he had her in his bed, Madeleine admitted that she was a virgin.

"It's rather simple," he explained. "Easier than A, B-"

"Sssh!" she said, impatient. "Let's get started."

The stranger spread her legs and entered her. Despite a little pain, she was thrilled. She never even missed her maidenhead. Instead, her hips met his as their breathing grew heavier. She was heading where she'd never been.

A ladder ahead. Her head was spinning. She was leaving the earth behind. Spiraling, levitating, jetting heavenward.

And then it happened. He hit her G-area.

"Ahh, Divine Being! *I'm arriving! I'm arriving!*"

That, dear reader, was Madeleine's answer.

Author's Note: The following letters were excluded from this tale: f, u, c, k, y, o.

Incantation by Eros

after Khlebnikov

O fuck it out, you fucksters!
O fuck it up, you fucksters!
So they fuck with fuckters,
so they fuckerize defuckly.
O fuck it up befuckably!
O the fuckamuck of the fucked-upon -
the fuck of befucked fucksters!
O fuck it out full-fuckingly, the fuck of
fucked-up fuckians!
Fuckerino, fuckerino,
Fuckify, fuckicate, fuckolets, fuckolets,
Fuckikins, fuckikins,
O fuck it out, you fucksters!
O fuck it up, you fucksters!

Reading for a Beautiful Bosom

Reading can be the key to a beautiful bosom, regardless of your size. Whether you are small, full-figured, or somewhere in between, a good program of reading can achieve several benefits for you. The first is to improve your posture. Reading while standing erect, a hardback held at arm's length from the chest, with shoulders relaxed, will help delineate a petite pair, raise a sagging bustline, and separate abundant orbs to minimize their size. The heavier the volume employed, the greater the benefits of chest-stretch. An oversized *Holy Bible* held with both hands at head level can firm up the bosom miraculously! Light-weight mass-market paperbacks – one in each hand – may be read (skimmed) alternately while turning the head from one to the other and lowering the arms upon completion of each page. Moreover, speed-reading a sentence from the left book to the right one, back and forth, until both pages of each volume have been digested for their gist — albeit combined — can tone up those pectoral muscles which support your breasts to give your bosom a higher, firmer, more intelligent appearance.

Another benefit of a carefully prepared program of reading: better proportions generally. Are your bosom and hip measurements nearly the same, your waist ten inches smaller? If not, try using a hardback and paperback simultaneously; juggle them over your head for ten minutes, then pause and speed-read a paragraph from either one. Switch books without losing your place. Now try to remember what you have read while placing the volumes under your arms and squeezing with your elbows. *Presto!* You will have brought those measurements into correct proportion.

Come on girls, start reading!

Tropic of Crater

Last night Judge Crater discovered the he was lousy. I had to shave his armpits and even then the itching did not stop. How can a judge get lousy in the tropics? But no matter. We might never have known each other so intimately, Crater and I, had it not been for the lice.

The weather has been lousy, too.

I was sent here three years ago to find hizzoner. The old coot had been missing since '30. Wanted by the Feds for questioning. Something to do with a slain dame named Tania. Her skull had been crushed by a blow from a Tibetan dildo. Hell of a weapon in the wrong hands. Blunt and to the point, if you catch my drift.

The first place I cased in my search for J.C. was a rundown little nosedive called Tiki's. Usual crowd of tropical lowlifes: a midget named Eddie; Delmore, a transvestite big-game hunter; Bobo, an oil company executive; and Buffy, a ventriloquist/prostitute with a reputation for throwing her voice during blow-jobs.

I stumbled up to the bar like a tinpot tourist in search of the sauce. I snapped on a smile for the benefit of the two-ton gorilla behind the counter who, eyeing my Burmudas and brand new Box Brownie, spat in my face.

Bulls-eye.

"Nice shot," I told him, wiping the scum from between my glims. "Does the name Judge Crater ring a bell?"

The big lug grinned but said nothing, just kept toweling the rim of a greasy mug. The silent treatment drove me nuts. I slid an 8x10 glossy across the bar. "Recognize the face?"

The truculent tender took a peek, then looked me square and, in the voice of a twelve year old girl, said, "Maybe. Maybe not." Then he threw me a curve in his regular tongue. "What's it to you, chump?"

I took a deep breath. "Well, you see, the Judge and me are old pals from way back and, uh, it's been ages since we've tied one on and, well, I wanted to ... invite him to a party!" I nodded for emphasis, but something in Tiki's laughter told me he wasn't buying. I tried another angle.

"Look, that was a lie. I lied to you. There is no party, at least not that I know of..." I cleared my throat. "Actually, I represent a big-time lawyer named, uh, Steinway, back in the States. Crater's grandmother just kicked the b. and left him a boatload of dough and ... he only has a week to claim it."

"Is that so?" smirked Tiki. "Then how come you have your fingers crossed?"

Good question. I quickly undid my digits.

"It's just a bad habit left over from boot camp."

The goon mused. "A lot of dough, eh? How much?"

I got the message.

"Okay, okay, you win..." I tossed down five clams. The owner shook his head. I added five more. "Now then, where do I find him?"

Tiki scooped up the moolah in his mitt and scratched his head. "Judge Crater, huh?... Hmm, let's see ..." He began tapping on the bar. "... two ... three... there's four. Which one you want?"

"What?"

"I know four judges named Crater," he said, nodding

at the photo, "but none of them have knockers like those."

I clutched back the glossy and there, to my amazement, was the face of Misty de La Motte, a stripper from Vegas, smiling up at me. Across her abundant chest was the following inscription: *To the sweetest Judge I know, love & kisses, Misty.*

"How the hell...?"

Then it dawned on me. Someone had pulled the old switcheroo.

I looked up at Tiki. "Sorry," I said sheepishly. "Wrong photo."

Suddenly, I felt fingers easing up my thigh.

I looked down to find a blonde on her knees, fondling my Bermudas and breathing a heat wave right where it counts. Then, in a voice that had to be hers but seemed to come from the overhead fan, she whispered, "Hello there, handsome, care for a *throw-job?*"

A dwarf at the end of the bar began bouncing up and down in a fit of glee. "Crazy box, eh boss? Me next! Me next!"

Tiki looked bored. "This bohunk ain't in a buyin' mood," he told her. "Unless the name *Crater* makes you sing."

At this, the blonde rose, smiling icicles, as the flames died down. The dwarf, however, was still plenty hot, shouting "now me, now me, boyoboy!" and banging his tiny fists on the bar.

I had to admit, the dame had a certain way about her. *My* way.

She tapped me on the shoulder and headed north. I shadowed her skirt to a booth in the back where the atmosphere took a dive. It was dark and musty and maybe unsafe. I watched as she slid her tail-section sideways on the seat, revealing enough thigh-white to set a preacher sinning Sundays.

I covered my erection with a wine list, then sat down across from her and turned on the charm.

"What's your tag, doll?" I queried. She seemed confused. "Your name. Like, what do they call you?"

"Oh, that's easy. Buffy. Everyone calls me Buffy. Except my ex." She frowned. "He calls me 'stupid bitch.'"

"I'm Miller, but Hank to you."

"Hanks to you, too," she giggled. "Hanky-panky-poo?"

"Later," I assured her, "but first I want to hear about the honorable Judge Crater."

She signaled to the bar with an out-stretched gam, then leaned in close, put her head in hands and sighed.

"Yeah, well, I knew him. He used to be a regular customer. A real weirdo."

"How so?"

The blonde turned red. "He was into TDs."

"Tee-vees?"

"No silly," scolded Buffy. "Tee-*dees*. Dee as in *dildo*." She smiled. "Tibetan dildos."

Things were beginning to add up.

She continued: "Real rough stuff, too."

"How rough is rough?"

Buffy shivered. "He threw me in front of a tractor."

It was then that I noticed the tread marks on her forehead.

Poor dumb broad.

"Sounds like my man, all right. Where does he hang his robe?"

She lit a cigar and puffed nervously. "In the boneyard, honey. He's dead."

If I'd had any dentures I'd have dropped them.

"Dead?!"

Buffy nodded. "Killed himself with a gavel."

It looked like the end of the line. I shook my head despondently.

"Don't pout," chirped Buffy, squeezing my paw. "He's not really dead. I was just teasing."

I gave her a sharp backhand across the chops.

Tiki arrived at our booth bearing a tray with two glasses, each filled with a queer blue concoction.

"Just in time," moaned the girl, rubbing her chin.

"On the house," winked the lummox, setting one drink down cautiously, like a time bomb, and handing the other directly to Buffy.

"What the hell is it?" I asked, peering into the murky blue haze, searching for signs of sea life.

"Try it," suggested Tiki, grinning. "It goes down real smooth."

He plodded back to his post, leaving me alone with the booze and the blonde. I knew either might be fatal. But, hell, that was my job. Danger every step of the way. Thrills, chills, and constipation. And all for what? Some two-bit bench-warmer on the lam? I wished I'd never heard of the bastard. Probably a wild goose chase anyhow.

"Come on," said Buffy, impatiently, "bottoms up." She raised the glass to her lips, waiting for me to join her. I did, and together, like a duo of drunks, we downed the elixir. The stuff had a funny taste but wasn't as strong as I feared.

"Kind of tart," I mumbled, pushing aside the empty. The dame looked hurt. Was it something I said? You can't figure dames.

The booze finally settled with a rumble in my gut. It

wasn't half bad. Hell, I'd had plenty worse in my day. It was working fast, too. My head felt hollow, horizontal, harpooned. I was suddenly seasick, riding the waves while Buffy – a blonde buoy – was bobbing out to sea. Her eyes were a tropical storm and I was sinking. Sinking fast. But before I hit bottom I heard a voice, a voice in that faraway froth ...

"It's all clear, Judge, you can come out now!"

Sexlus

A Neutered text, after Henry Miller

I said it had a marvelous physique. It was full and supple, limber, smooth as a seal. When I ran my hands over its lower portion it was enough to make me forget all my problems – even Nietzsche. As for its thing, if it wasn't exactly beautiful, it was attractive and arresting. Perhaps its thing was a trifle worn-out, but it suited its personality. Of course there was nothing more to it than what you could see or touch. Its personality was as much in its left thing, so to speak, as in its little right thing. It was not perfect – not by a long shot – but it was provocative. It had no need to flaunt or fling it about. In fact, one could say it was quite content ... happy just being *it*.

Terry Southern's Lollipops (¡)

Being a compilation of all 80 exclamation marks*—(sans text)—found among the 4,799 words contained in 100 paragraphs comprising the notorious "hunchback" section of the emphatically pornographic novel, Candy. *The book is legendary for its inordinate use of exclamations throughout and may explain why it was also released briefly under the title* Lollipop.

[* The longest stretch between exclamations in this excerpt runs a remarkable 351 words! For this, the author deserves high praise indeed.]

!

!

!

!

!

!

!

!

!

!

!

!

!

!   !

!

!   !

!   !   !

!

!

!

!

!

!

!

!   !   !

!

!

!

!

!

!

!

!

!

!

!

!

!

!

!

!

!

!

!

!

!

!

!

!

!

!   !

!

!

!

!　　!　　　　　　!　　　　　!

!

!

!

!

.

!　　　　　　　!

!　　!

! ! !   ! ! ! ! !   ! !
/   !

!

Lolita, Over the Hill

Lolita.

Lo-lee-ta. Lo. Lee. Tah. Lohhhh-leee-tuhhhh...

Old Granny Lo. Old in the morning and ancient at dusk. She was Lola in her pediatric shoes. She was Dolly at the bingo hall. She was Dolores at the nursing home. But in my dreams she was always Lolita.

Lo. Lee. Tah.

Poor old Lo; insecure on Social Security, surviving on cat food (tuna and liver). Dark-stained dentures. Wheelchair and cane. Victim of the budget axe, the door-to-door con-men, the connivers, punks and purse-snatchers. Lola all alone in her creaky solitude. Solo-Lolita, aged orphan in the storm, awaiting a meal-on-wheels. Counting the days, the hyphens. Lee-*tahh*.

In her rocker, or off it, talking softly to herself. Cursing the years, ungrateful sons and daughters. Crusty old Lo-lee-ta, lost in the Pepsi Generation's maze, rocking slowly out to seed ...

"It's Humbert Jr., remember me?"

"Wha?"

Deaf, too, my darling. My silent, lonely Lee-taa. Lo and behold, had I the will to hold you, Lo — *yo!* — Leetaa! I shouted my name in her pale left ear. She sighed and drifted off to sleep. Sleepy Lo, my Lolabye.

Lola sleeps in dreamy deeps. Now gone to earth and far away.

Goodbye, my Lolita, goodbye.

Naked Lunch at Tiffany's

I am always drawn back to neighborhoods where I have lived – for instance Queens Plaza, where I had my first apartment. The date palms have died of meat lack, the well filled with dried shit and mosaic of a thousand newspapers. Johnny dowses Mary with gasoline from an obscene Chimu jar of white jade. Even so my spirits heightened.

It never occurred to me in those days to write about Holly Golightly, a thin wholesome American cunt.

Holly Golightly had been a tenant on the roof of Nedick's. One night it was long past twelve, I woke up at the sound of Doctor Benway calling down the stairs, exasperated and stern. "Miss Golightly! You cheap Factualist bitch!"

The voice that came back, welling up from the bottom of the stairs, was silly-young and self-amused. "Oh, darling, I'm sorry. I'll go wash my ass. So there I was completely out of K.Y. in the headwaters of the Baboon's asshole … "

"Shut up you fool. Bitch marry so many times so many gooks and spics she don't know her accent from her ass!"

"Oh, don't be angry, you dear little man. And if you promise not to be angry" — her voice was coming nearer, she was climbing the stairs — "I might let you palpate my internal hemorrhoids."

Doctor Benway's face swelled, tumescent with blood. His lips turned purple.

Holly smiled. "The next time a girl wants a little powder-room change, take my advice, darling: fuck her in no gravity. Your jism just floats out in the air like lovely ectoplasm, and females are subject to immaculate conception ... Reminds me of an old friend of mine, Rusty Trawler, one of the handsomest men I have ever known and absolutely ruined by wealth. He used to go about with a water pistol shooting jism up career women at parties. Won all his paternity suits hands down. He never used his own jism you understand."

The following afternoon I could feel the heat closing in, feel them out there making their moves. I was just tying up for my morning shot when in burst Golightly, the spit hanging off her chin like rancid semen.

"Darling!" she cried. "Turn over, I'll give it to you in the ass."

A kicking junky can make a whole apartment stink with a death smell. "No thanks, I can do it myself."

"Look what I just bought," she beamed, thrusting two rubber cocks in my face. "I just had to buy some little something. They're from *Tiffany's*."

Maybe writing about Holly wasn't such a hot idea after all.

Anaïs Nin's
Architecture of Desire

Anaïs climbed the solid masonry placed to counteract the lateral thrust of the vault. In the distance she thought she could see the citadel of a Greek city built at its highest point and containing the chief temples and public buildings, as at Athens. 'But I'm in Los Angeles,' thought Anaïs. At first the rich smell of unburnt brick drying in the sun, the other worldly sanctuary of this Greek temple, the condo apartments below and the thickness and silence of the surrounding structures on which sacrificial offerings are placed, were all she could grasp of the environment she was entering.

'I must remember to record this in my diary.'

Alvar Aalto, among the most important living architects (and certainly pre-eminent in his native Finland), led Anaïs to a platform in the center of a range of arches carried on piers and plastered with advertising posters. He directed her to sit down where there would normally have been a raised panel below the window-sill, but there was no window. 'Henry,' she thought, 'up to his old tricks again.' She leaned back against a short pillar that supported a coping and thus formed a balustrade. She could see nothing beyond the platform's walls and the intricate and fanciful decorations that appeared in a vaporous neon glow-cloud that drifted through the gloomy shadows of palm trees. It made no difference to her, as she was exhausted from the climb and preoccupied with the next entry in her little black book. Indeed, Alvar was quite an architectural wonder in his own Wright.

Presently, Benedetto Antelami, a sculptor and most probably an architect, too, joined Anaïs on the platform, having just come from a seedy little cinema on Sepulveda where *The House of Usher* had played to a packed house of building inspectors. He reached up to inspect the continuous architrave moulding above her head. His fingers gently caressed the surface, as if it were the body of a statue he himself had sculpted. 'He grabbed me in his arms ...' mused Anaïs, her heart all aflutter in the poetry of the moment. Then, as Antelami leaned closer, she tried to think of something intelligent to ask that would please him. Maybe she should show an interest in his work.

But before she could speak, two architects from her past — Diogo Arruda and Charles Robert Ashbee — pushed aside the imitation velvet curtains that separated Anaïs from the steaming streets of L.A. She noted at a glance the graceless, conventional clothes that stamped them immediately as architects while they sedately planted themselves down on a fixed wooden seat in the aisle. At the same time, Alvar Aalto entered and stood beside the balustrade. He had read of these creatures in Anaïs Nin's diary.

"I despise you both," hissed Aalto, "and everything you represent."

Anaïs turned to him now, admiring his amber-colored suit. She judged Aalto to be elegant and well-bred (possibly loaded), qualities that are not usually associated with natives of Finland. She tried to guess his age as he wrestled with Arruda and Ashbee on the ledge. Eighty? Ninety? Perhaps even older. The poor fellow didn't have a chance.

He was hurled to his death in the smog below.
"The traffic is heavy tonight," smiled Ashbee.
'I must remember that line,' thought Anaïs.

Query of Venus

A Rhetorical Text for Anaïs Nin

Was Mathilde a hat maker in Paris? Was she barely twenty when she was seduced by the Baron? Did the affair not last more than two weeks? If not, in that short time, did she somehow become imbued (by contagion?) with his philosophy of life? Was she intrigued by something the Baron may have asked her casually one night? — Were Parisian women highly prized in South America because of (a) their expertness in matters of love; (b) their vivaciousness and wit; or (c) none of the above?

Like the Baron, did Mathilde develop a formula for acting out life as a series of roles (assuming this was, in fact, the Baron's formula)? That is, did she ask herself in the morning while brushing her blonde hair, 'Do I want to become this or that person?' and then proceed to become one of those people?

Did she decide one day to become an elegant representative of a well-known Parisian modiste and go to Peru? Was acting out the role all she had to do? If so, did she present herself with extraordinary assurance at the house of the modiste who gave her a boat ticket to Lima?

Was she aboard ship and did she behave like a French missionary of elegance? Did her innate talent for recognizing good wines, good perfumes, good dressmaking, mark her as a lady of refinement? Was her palate that of a gourmet? Was it her laugh that attracted the Spanish Line representative, Dalvedo, who perhaps invited her to sit at the captain's table? Did Dalvedo look suave in his evening suit? Did he take her to dance the next night? At midnight, did he ask her if she liked cactus figs? Had she ever tasted them? Did he say he had some in his cabin?

Was she on her guard when she entered the cabin? Had she easily rebuffed the audacious hands of the men she brushed against when marketing? Did the husbands of her clients slyly pat her buttocks? Did male friends invite her to the movies and pinch her nipples? Did none of this stir her? Had she a vague but tenacious idea of what could stir her? Did she want to be courted with mysterious language? Had this been determined by her first adventure?

Did a writer, who was a celebrity in Paris, enter her shop one day? Was he looking for a hat?

Did he ask if she sold luminous flowers? Did he say he wanted them for a woman who shone in the dark? Could he swear that when he took her to the theatre that her skin had a pale pink glow to it?

And did he want these flowers for her to wear in her hair?

Did Mathilde have them?

Did the man leave?

Did he come back?

Did Mathilde's heart beat so swiftly that she felt her story was drawing to a climax?

Did the writer ask her in his aristocratic voice, "Was I stiff in my pants as soon as I saw you?"

Were his words crude? Were they an insult to her?

Did she redden and strike him?

Was this scene repeated on several occasions?

Now was she back in the cabin of the smooth Spaniard, Dalvedo? Was Dalvedo peeling some cactus figs for her? Did he rise and ask, "Do you have a little mole on your chin that is most seductive?" Did she think he would try to kiss her? Did he or didn't he? Did he unbutton himself quickly, take out his penis and ask her to kneel?

Did she strike him and move towards the door?

Did he beg her not to go? Did he try to embrace her and did she struggle to elude him?

And, last but not least, did she ever arrive in Lima and attain her dream?

Is this the beginning or the end?

The Ravishing of Lol V. Stein

with Marguerite Duras

The weather is beautiful. But Lol, contrary to custom, has shut the bay windows in the living room. When we reached the darkened house, with its open windows, we heard a soft tittering. If that doesn't make sense, read on.

Lol has shared with Tatiana another ribald anecdote. We heard their muffled laughter echoing on the floor above. And then they came back downstairs to the living room. We were already in the billiard room. I assumed Lol was amused to find us gone. I heard her hoarse laugh as she shut the three bay windows.

She, on the other side of the vestibule, and I, here in the game room, whose floor I am pacing, are waiting to see each other again.

It was an odd play. The women laughed a lot. On three occasions, Lol and Tatiana were the only ones laughing. During intermission, I overheard several people gossiping about Lol.

I leave the billiard room. Lol is seated facing the bay window, giggling to herself, as usual. She does not yet see me. The living room is smaller than the billiard room, and is furnished with an untold number — who's counting? — of matching easy chairs.

Lol gets up unsteadily and offers Tatiana a glass of sherry. She, Lol, is not yet drinking for she is still consumed by some private joke – doubled up, as it were. Tatiana seems to be on the verge of cracking up. She is speaking gibberish, then breaks off into guffaws. She makes a face at Lol who belly laughs and begins rolling on the floor. She was obviously hearing punch lines again.

Now she has us all in stitches.

Why? How? I have no idea.

I will not be meeting Tatiana at the asylum until the day after tomorrow, yes – don't laugh – two days from now. I would like to make it tonight, after we leave Lol's. I have a feeling that tonight my desire for Tatiana will be sated forever, the task accomplished, however arduous, long, and painfully difficult it may be.

Lol gets up now, says something foolish, hoots and grins at Tatiana who steps back in mock horror. Lol lunges at her and gently strokes her hair, sniggering. Tatiana chuckles. Lol bursts out laughing.

Up until that very minute, I tried to comprehend what was going on between them – thought, perhaps, I might be able to make some sense of it all – but it was hopeless.

Lol is still laughing, stroking Tatiana's hair. At first she gazes at her teasingly, then dissolves into hysterics again. For her part, Tatiana has regained her composure and is staring vacantly into space.

Lol rolls her eyes, and I can see her lips trembling as she attempts to form the name: *Tatiana Karl*. She is suppressing another eruption.

Admittedly the name was an unfortunate choice. Don't blame me, it wasn't mine. Marguerite Duras made her messy bed and must lie in it. As for me? I couldn't care less.

* * *

Suddenly, here are their voices, interwoven, diluted by the night, spiked with laughter, similarly feminine giggles which seem but one voice by the time they reach my ears. I can hear both of them. That is what Lol wanted.

I discover them by the bay window in the library.

"Look at all these trees," says Lol, "these absurd trees of ours. I find them utterly ridiculous."

Tatiana raises an eyebrow. "Tell me, Lol, which one do you find the funniest?"

"The weeping willow, naturally."

Tatiana gives a long, plaintive, weary sigh. Even she has reached her wit's end.

Lol shoots me a grin, then makes an obscene gesture and roars with laughter.

"What is so goddamned funny?" I scream.

Lol stares at me, straight-faced for a long moment, and then a smile creeps across her lips.

"You can't be serious," she says. "Why, you're even stupider than you look."

"I don't get it!"

Lol opens the window and climbs out onto the lawn.

"Google my name, you idiot."

I join Tatiana and together we watch as Lol walks away.

We stand there waiting until, *finally*, we hear her laugh out loud.

Thérèse and Isabelle

The air was heavy, the air was barbaric.

Isabelle was preparing to stab me.

"I bleed very easily."

"Be quiet, Thérèse."

"Isabelle ..." I closed my eyes.

"Wipe away the saliva."

"No."

Isabelle slapped me. She pulled my hair.

"You're hurting me, my love ..." We bumped against packing crates full of crockery. We fell onto the steps. Isabelle sat on my knees. She slapped me again.

"Don't stop. That's it, that's it."

"I really want to strangle you," she screamed, "I really do."

"I'll do whatever you want," I said.

"The saliva ... wipe away the saliva."

"I can't." I was being sadistic. "Not here, not now."

"I'm taking you to see a doctor," she said.

I imagined her talking to me under her breath in the darkness of the dormitory. The gentle tingling of an ambulance bell punctuated our ecstasies.

"If I had leprosy," I whispered, "would you leave me?"

Isabelle stood up. She ground her teeth.

"Yes!"

I jumped up, threw the lid of my slop pail onto the floor and went into battle. I pushed her up against the wall. I stormed her, hoping to plunder and destroy her.

"Blood ... I saw some blood!"

I staggered. Isabelle gripped me with a scissor movement of her legs. "I'm trapped," I said.

Soon I would be vomiting. My efforts, my sweat, my rhythm were exciting me. Maybe I should see a doctor after all.

"You're biting!" cried Isabelle.

She had moved around to my back, circled me with one arm, dragged me, slapped me, pulled those sullen hanks of hair while I tore at her pinafore.

"We are unsociable, aren't we?"

I seized her leg in my arms and pulled.

"Do you still love me?" I begged.

"What are you doing? Take away your hands!"

I abandoned her. I ran to and fro across the room, I wondered whether I'd have the strength to ever write this story.

"Where are you?" she asked.

The darkness suited me. I waited by the window. We waited for one another, sensing the crevasse of terror that lay between us.

"Come."

"It's too dangerous," said Isabelle.

I took her by the hand and led her to the window.

"What is there to be afraid of? ... Lean over."

We heard the wind flapping in the shroud of a tree.

"Lean over," I repeated.

"No, no .. .I shall die."

I couldn't bring myself to do it. She let go of my hand. She fell back.

Isabelle was falling.

I lost all notion of time. The day was taking the night,

the day was erasing our couplings with its own. Already there were birds clustering in a tree and pecking at the first glimmers of day.

I never saw Isabelle again.

HER LOVER ONE DAY TAKES O FOR A WALK IN A SECTION OF THE CITY WHERE THEY NEVER GO – MONTSOURIS PARK.

AFTER THEY HAVE TAKEN A STROLL, AND HAVE SAT TOGETHER SIDE BY SIDE ON THE EDGE OF A LAWN, THEY NOTICE, AT THE CORNER OF THE PARK, A CAR WHICH, BECAUSE OF ITS METER, RESEMBLES A TAXI.

"GET IN," HE SAYS.
"NO," SAYS O.

© 2013
DEREK PELL &
DOUG SKINNER

Story of O

An Expurgated Version,
Tastefully Rearranged

In the wee hours of the night, just before dawn when it is darkest and coldest, Pierre reappeared. The sun had broken through the mist and flooded the room. But only the midday bell woke them. He did not leave until he saw that her eyes were clear and her expression calm, contented. O wept, and did not fall asleep until dawn. Jeanne took O by the hand and led her out into the hallway.

"Don't wear me out completely, I have to be up early tomorrow."

O had never been to the South of France before. She fell asleep.

The music had begun again, the dancers were dancing again. O worked in the fashion department. She had always been a conservative dresser.

"Please be good enough to turn around," he said.

The tears streamed down into her open mouth.

"I was just going to start ... but I got up late, took a bath, and it was noon before I was ready."

As a child, O had read a Biblical text. She was waiting for an order. It came to her not from René, but from Sir Stephen.

"Go into the front bedroom over there."

But O was afraid of making a fool of herself.

"No, it's out of the question."

The dog barked faintly when the bell rang: a big, shaggy

sheep dog that sniffed at O's knees. O followed him to the car, climbed in, and sat down. It was hard to tell whether she was proud of this or not, whether or not she considered this the first step in a career which might lead to her becoming famous.

Story of O x 2

A redundant text

O ne day her lover — the man with whom she sleeps — takes O for a walk in a section of the city where they never go — Montsouris Park. O and her lover have never been to Montsouris Park, a section of the city that seems quite foreign to them. After they have taken a stroll in the park, walked slowly around the manicured lawn, strolling arm in arm as lovers are given to do in Paris — and have sat together side by side — that is to say, next to each other — on the edge of this lawn — they notice — both seeing at the same instant — at one corner of the park (the northeast edge of the park to their left, to be precise) — at an intersection where there are never any taxis (of course, they don't know there are never any taxis at the intersection since they haven't been to Montsouris Park before, but there are, in fact, *never* any taxis) — a car — an automobile of indeterminate make and model, which, because of its meter resembles a taxi.

How odd.

Stranger still, since there are never any taxis at the intersection. (I would reveal the cross-street but am unable to make it out from this distance.) Of course it might not be a taxi after all, simply a car with a meter attempting to look like a taxi in a place where there never are any. Thus, either O or her lover (or both of them) may have assumed it was a taxi. Then again, they may not have. But with its meter running it certainly looked like one. Trust me.

"Get in," he says. "Step inside this vehicle that resembles a taxi, and while you're at it, watch your head."

"I will watch my head as I step inside this vehicle that resembles a taxi," she says, watching her head as she steps inside the vehicle that resembles a taxi. She doesn't bang her head, of course, as she was being exceedingly cautious since her lover had warned her in advance to watch her head. Had he not done so, she would undoubtedly have banged her head. Furthermore, it goes without saying that people will watch their heads whenever anyone tells them to watch their heads.

"Are you in the vehicle that resembles a taxi?" he asks.

"I'm in the backseat of the vehicle that resembles a taxi, yes I am," O assures him.

"Are you certain?" he says.

O gives him a look.

"Good. I'm glad you've managed to get inside the vehicle that resembles a taxi without bumping your head. We'll save the pain for later."

"Hurry up," sighs O, "the meter is running."

* * *

It is autumn, late October, and coming up to dusk. About 6 o'clock. It gets dark at around six here. She is dressed as she always is: high heels, a suit with a pleated skirt, stockings, a silk blouse, panties, gloves, and no hat. She wears the same outfit every day, no matter where she goes. Stilettos, suit, skirt, stockings, panties, gloves and a white silk blouse. Nothing else. Not even a hat when it rains. Just long gloves which come up over the sleeves of her jacket. (Did I mention the jacket?), and in her leather handbag she has her identification papers, her compact, and her lipstick. She rummages with gloved hands through the leather purse making sure everything is there: lipstick (check), compact (check), i. d. (check).

The vehicle resembling a taxi moves off slowly, crawls through the intersection like a snail, the man still not having said a word to the driver. (Yes, there is a driver, too.) The driver drives in silence since the man in the backseat has yet to address him and, perhaps, never will. Maybe the man has a grudge against the driver and refuses to talk to him. Or maybe he's just the strong silent type. He does, however, pull down the shades of the windows on both sides of the vehicle resembling a taxi, and the shade on the back window. He makes certain all the shades are drawn, and they are.

O has taken off her gloves, removed them both, one at a time, thinking he wants to kiss her or that he wants her to caress him. So she removed each glove, one at a time, seductively, in the manner of a striptease artist. *He probably intends to kiss me,* is what she is thinking to herself. Then again, he may simply want her to service him while he leans back and ignores the driver of the car resembling a taxi. But instead he says: "Your bag is in your way; let me have it. The leather handbag in your lap. Give it to me, it's in your way."

She rolls her eyes but hands it to him. She gives him the bag just like he asked her to, pretending it's an encumbrance. He puts it out of her reach, he stuffs it under the front seat where she can't readily grasp it. When it's hidden under the seat in front of them, he says: "You also have on too many clothes. Unfasten your stockings and roll them down to above your knees. Here are some garters. Why do you wear so many clothes? Get undressed ... leave the stockings as I said rolled above the knees."

By now the vehicle resembling a taxi has picked up speed, the driver accelerating in order to go faster, and she has some trouble managing her lover's request for the taxi (if, that, in fact, is what it is) is exceeding the speed limit and she is being jostled about due to the bumps in the road, so it's hard to comply with the instructions without appearing clumsy and somewhat ridiculous. Bouncing about like a doll, head bobbing. She is also afraid the driver of the vehicle resembling a taxi will turn around. Any moment, the driver might turn and glance over his shoulder and see her. Why, he might even glance in the rearview mirror which, under the circumstances, would make more sense. How embarrassing if he were to get an eyeful.

Finally, though, the stockings are rolled down as her lover had instructed, and she's embarrassed to feel her legs naked and free beneath her silk slip. Besides, the loose garter-belt suspenders are slipping back and forth. Back and forth they slip, slip, slip.

"Unfasten your garter belt," he says, "and take off your panties."

That's easy enough; all she has to do is slip her hands behind her back and raise herself slightly. So she does — she slips her hands behind herself and raises herself and removes the garter belt and panties in one fell swoop. Off they go.

He takes the garter belt and panties from her, reaches under the front seat, removes her leather handbag, opens it, puts them inside, returns the bag to its former position under the seat, then says: "You shouldn't sit on your slip and skirt. Pull them up behind you and sit directly on the seat."

So she pulls up her slip and skirt and puts them behind her and is suddenly in direct contact with the seat. The seat is made of some sort of imitation leather — Naugahyde, perhaps — which is slippery, sticky and cold. It's quite an extraordinary sensation to feel the seat sticking to her thighs. If it were real leather — like her handbag — it would probably feel different and not be so sticky. A little sticky, maybe, but not so much.

Then he says: "Now put your gloves back on. Both of them. Put them on so they cover your hands."

The vehicle resembling a taxi is still moving along at a rapid clip, and she doesn't dare ask why René just sits there without moving or saying another word, nor can she guess what all this means to him – having her there motionless, silent, so stripped and exposed, so thoroughly gloved, in the backseat of a black vehicle which resembles a taxi going God knows where. Even He — the Almighty — hasn't a clue where they're going. On second thought, perhaps He does.

René hasn't told her what to do or what not to do for several minutes, which isn't like him at all. She is unsure what she should do now. She's afraid either to cross her legs or press them together. She sits with her gloved hands braced on either side of her seat. She doesn't do anything because he hasn't told her to do anything.

"Here we are," he announces suddenly. The vehicle resembling a taxi stops on a lovely avenue, beneath a tree — they are plane trees — in front of some sort of small private home which can be seen nestled between the courtyard and the garden, the type of small private dwelling one finds along the Faubourg Saint-Germain. The vehicle resembling a taxi is parked now. Not moving. The engine is silent. The street lamps are some distance away, and it is still fairly dark inside the car since René hasn't put the shades back up. Outside it is raining.

"Listen," he says. "Now you're ready. This is where I leave you. You're to get out of this vehicle resembling a taxi and go ring the doorbell of that small private home." He gestures toward the small private home. "There's a button on the left side of the front door and you simply press it with your finger. Like this..." He demonstrates by pressing an imaginary button. "It will ring inside the small private home and they'll hear it and someone will come to the door and open the door."

O smiles. "I think I know what happens next," she says.

René arches an eyebrow. "You do?"

She nods. "The door of the small private home will open and I will step inside out of the rain. And then, whomever opened the door will shut it behind me, and I'll be inside the small private dwelling which looks like a house on the Faubourg Saint-Germain." She looks him in the eye. "Do you want me to go on? There's more..."

"No," he says, "that's quite enough. Get out."

Without a word O gets out of the vehicle resembling a taxi and walks up to the front door of the small private dwelling which resembles a house on the Faubourg Saint-Germain. The wind is blowing. The rain is heavy as the vehicle resembling a taxi drives off. O watches it go, then turns and stares at the doorknob.

Time passes into night.

O stands waiting in the darkness.

Her hand does not reach out, nor does she press the button. She has simply forgotten to ring the bell.

RAYMOND QUENEAU'S STORY OF O

5 + 5

÷ 2

- 5

=

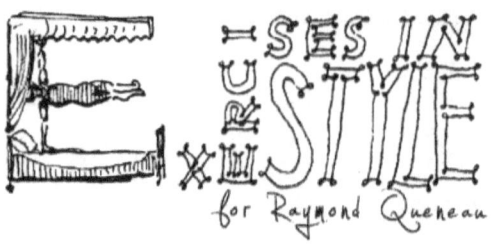

At the back of the S bus, in the rush hour, a lady of about 26, placed a finger in her vagina and squeezed her muscles. She could feel the muscles tightening and her pelvic floor rising up. She imagined she was trying to hold back urine; she lifted and squeezed from the inside. She attempted to hold that action for the count of three. Then she imagined she was trying to stop herself from passing wind. She lifted and squeezed her anus and held for a count of three. She combined these two movements into one fluid movement. Starting from the front, she lifted and squeezed and didn't let go, following through to her anus, lifted and squeezed. She relaxed and held her position for approximately 10 seconds. This routine was repeated several times until the bus came to a stop and she got off.

Emmanuelle

A Definitive Text

Emmanuelle's joints between the thighbone and the lower part of the human leg were bare in the golden something that makes things visible or affords illumination. Under the invisible elastic synthetic material used in hosiery and textiles, the movement of their small hollow areas made agile dark figures or images cast on a surface by a body intercepting light in the toasted-brown quality of an object or substance with respect to light reflected by it, of their external covering of an animal body. She knew the excited state or condition they caused. They seemed more naked than ever under the strong, focused light thrown upon a particular person or object, as on a stage, which had been turned on them. She felt as if she were coming out of the transparent, odorless, tasteless liquid which constitutes rain, oceans, lakes, etc. after a moonlight period of swimming. Her flattened region on each side of the forehead in human beings throbbed faster and her two fleshy folds forming the margins of the mouth filled with the fluid that circulates in the vascular system of humans and other vertebrates. She closed her organs of sight and saw herself, not partially but totally naked, and she knew that once again she would be helpless against the act of tempting or seduction of that narcissistic meditation on spiritual things.

A complete absence of something else happened for some duration of all existence, past, present and future. She then became aware that his terminal part of the upper limb below the wrist was lifting the large piece of soft fabric used as a covering for warmth and drawing it aside. When it touched her bare external covering of animal body she started for the first duration of all existence, past, present, and future, and tried to break the irresistible influence. Then the terminal part of his upper limb below the wrist forced the segments of her legs or hind limbs between the knee and the trunk to spread further apart. It closed over her warm, swollen organ of reproduction, caressing it as if to soothe it, without swiftness of motion, following the narrow groove made in the ground, esp. by a plow, of its two fleshy folds forming the margins of the mouth, dipping lightly between them, passing over the erect small organ at the upper part of the vulva, homologous to the penis in the male, and coming to rest on the thick coils or ringlets of hair of the pan of the innominate bone that forms the front of the pelvis. As they moved to and fro between the limbs of animals and human beings that support and move the body, the terminal members of the hand, esp. those other than the thumb, sank deeper between her moist, pliable layers of animal or vegetable tissue serving to line an organ or connect parts, slowing their advance, and seeming to hesitate as her act of stretching or straining increased. Biting her two fleshy folds forming the margins of the mouth to stifle the sigh, cry or wail accompanied by a convulsive catching of the breath that was rising from her passage from the mouth to the stomach or to the lungs, she panted with an intense longing as the adult male human being brought her closer and closer to the culmination of a sexual act without letting her reach it.

Then his terminal part of the upper limb below the wrist stopped moving and cupped the whole part of her physical structure and substance of an animal or plant that it had inflamed. He leaned toward her, extended his other terminal part of the upper limb below the wrist, took one of hers and drew it inside his two-legged outer garment worn chiefly by men and boys, extending from the hips to the ankles. He helped her to grasp his rigid male organ of urination and copulation and guided her acts or processes of moving.

When his satisfied male organ of urination and copulation finally disgorged its fluid produced in the male reproductive organs, containing spermatozoa, in long white, odorous, sudden, forceful gushes or jets, as of liquid, she received it with strange abnormal intensification of a mental state or of the power of an organ or function, esp., an abnormal sense of personal well-being, power or importance, along her upper limbs of the human body, on her bare abdomen or abdominal cavity, on her part of the neck in front of the spinal column, hence the passage through it containing the pharynx and the upper part of the esophagus, the larynx, and the trachea, her front part of the head, and the opening through which an animal or human takes in food or utters sounds, and in her fine cylindrical filaments growing from the skin of humans and animals. It seemed that it would never stop.

Later, she looked for him among the persons who are carried in a public or private conveyance when they had gotten off the heavier-than-air aircraft kept aloft by the upward thrust exerted by the passing air on its fixed wings and driven by propellers, jet propulsion, etc. But she saw no one as tall as he. The woman who works as a steward, esp. one who works as a flight attendant, smiled at her, but Emmanuelle scarcely noticed her. She was already being pushed toward the moveable structures closing an opening in a fence or wall. Emmanuelle ran forward with a cry of joy and threw herself into the outstretched upper limbs of her man who has a wife.

Ménage à trois

At the end of the last session Claire informed me that in the future I could have little Anne whenever I wanted her, and could amuse myself with her however I pleased.

—Jean de Berg
The Image

I wanted Anne. I wanted her close. I wanted the future with her. However, the session with Claire pleased little Anne. Could I amuse her myself whenever I wanted? Anne pleased her at the last session. And Claire pleased me. I wanted Anne whenever Claire wanted her. Could I have Anne amuse her whenever Claire wanted her to have me? Claire informed me that I could amuse myself in the future, at the close of the last session, whenever. I, however, wanted little of Claire and that pleased Anne. Whenever I wanted Anne, Claire could have her and whenever Claire wanted Anne ... Anne wanted me. However, I wanted Anne myself. At the last session Claire wanted her. However, I wanted Claire at the last session. I wanted Claire, Claire wanted Anne, and Anne wanted Claire. In the future Anne wanted me with Claire. I could have her whenever Claire wanted. I informed Claire that I wanted Anne myself. I wanted to have her whenever I could. Claire could amuse her whenever Anne wanted, however, I could have the last session with Claire whenever I pleased.

Could the future with Anne last? Could Claire have wanted me at the last session?

Whenever I wanted Claire in the future I could have

Anne with her. However I could amuse Claire myself. Anne could amuse me whenever Claire pleased her. Could I have pleased myself with Claire and Anne in the session? I could have, however I wanted Anne last. And Claire wanted the last of me. Anne, however, wanted little of me in the future. I informed Claire that I wanted Anne. Claire could have her whenever Anne wanted. I wanted little of Claire and Claire was pleased. I wanted Anne. Anne wanted me. Anne pleased me whenever I wanted, and I pleased Anne. However, in the future, Claire could have me whenever I wanted Claire.

And, at last, I pleased myself.

Position of Parts

She is lying on her right side, the upper part of her body half flung back so as to turn her face up into the camera. The right arm is stretched the length of her body while the left arm is raised over head hiding the ear but giving a good view of the downy armpit and the breast. The legs are bent, the right one slightly and the left much more, the knee pulled way up. From the way the picture was taken and the lighting, one can clearly see the inside of the right thigh, the buttocks, the lower pubic region and all the surrounding tender flesh.

—Jean de Berg, with shades of Robbe-Grillet
The Image

The legs are flung back over her head and stretched the length of her body so that the inside of the right thigh is raised over the left armpit. The right arm is bent slightly so as to turn the left ear into the right thigh over the raised left armpit from the back. The downy buttocks are pulled way up and to the left and flung over the upper part of the right breast, hiding the inside of the upper left half of her slightly stretched lower pubic region. The raised left arm is bent to the right of the legs and pulled to the back of her head over the right ear. The right arm is stretched up over the left knee while the right knee is hiding the left half of her bent head from the region inside the lower part of the right half of her left arm. The raised right arm is taken back inside the stretched legs while the right knee is pulled up over the slightly bent right thigh and stretched inside the lower right armpit and left lying on the downy upper part of the tender left thigh. The buttocks are flung up and to the right so that the lower left half is raised over the surrounding upper right region of her body, while the lower inside right thigh is hiding the face from the left side of the right breast. Her head is stretched slightly back from the inside of the left thigh and raised to the right of the lower left arm. The legs are bent more to the right so as to turn the face up into the buttocks hiding the left ear. The right arm is pulled way up over the left thigh giving a good view of the right knee from inside the left armpit on the right side of the raised left knee. The lower back is bent, while the legs are pulled up from the right arm over the left breast surrounding the buttocks from over the head. The left side of the lower pubic region is pulled way up and left lying on the upper part of the slightly stretched right breast. If the lighting is good, the tender flesh is clearly seen from inside the camera.

$9\frac{1}{2}$ Weeks: The Long March

The first time we were in bed together he held my hands pinned down above my head.

"Some works," he explained, "distort the historical facts."

He was moody in a way that struck me as romantic.

"Some works describe heroic characters," he told me softly, strengthening his grip on my wrists. " ... characters who always violate discipline ... or create heroes only to make them die in an artificially tragic ending. Some works do not present heroic characters but only middle characters who are actually backward people, caricatures of workers, peasants or soldiers. In depicting the enemy, they fail to expose his class nature as an exploiter and oppressor of the people, and even go so far as to prettify him."

"You're hurting me," I said.

"Then," he continued, ignoring me, his voice husky and passionate, "there are works, such as this, concerned only with love and romance, pandering to philistine tastes and claiming that love and death are eternal themes. All such bourgeois, revisionist trash must be resolutely opposed!"

He was funny, too.

"All reactionaries are paper tigers."

He was always saying funny stuff like that.

He was big and bright and interesting to talk to. He gave me pleasure, he gave me pain.

"Works of art which lack artistic quality have no force, however progressive they are politically. Therefore ..." He paused to pinch my flesh. "... I oppose both works of art with a wrong political viewpoint and the tendency towards the poster and slogan style which is correct in political viewpoint but lacks in artistic power."

The second time we were together he picked up my scarf from the floor where I had dropped it while getting undressed, smiled, and said "Would you let me blindfold you? The people's state protects the people." No one had blindfolded me in bed before and I liked it. I liked him even better than the first night and later couldn't stop smiling during my period of self-criticism. I had found an extraordinarily skillful lover.

"You're an extraordinarily skillful lover."

He shook his head. "Helmsman," he corrected.

The third time he repeatedly brought me within a hairs-breadth of coming. He would stop and exclaim, "To link oneself with the masses, one must act in accordance with the needs and wishes of the masses!"

When I was beside myself yet again and he stopped once more, I heard my voice disembodied above the bed ...

"Most worshipped and beloved leader, I will struggle to defeat all bourgeois intellectuals."

The fourth time, when I had mastered the basic principles of Marxism and felt comfortable with hyperbole, he used the same scarf to tie my wrists together.

"You must preserve the style of plain living and hard struggle."

Yes, he was hard and we struggled constantly. It seemed as if March would never end. The weeks wore on and became an arduous blur. I no longer even knew my own name.

He raised the whip and smiled.

"Art and literature must operate as powerful weapons

for uniting and educating the people and for attacking and destroying the enemy."

He attacked and destroyed me, night after night. Until, finally, nine and a half weeks later, spring arrived, along with thirteen copies of a little red book.

A writer, eh? I should have known.

The Sexual Life of Catherine M.

The line is longer than my ex-husband's penis. It stretches for blocks and I'm stuck at the end. *Oh balls!* There must be at least 150 people ahead of me. I could shoot myself for not bringing a book. But then who wants to be seen reading Proust at an orgy. I assure you I am *not* a wallflower – not by a long shot of semen across the bow – yet, sadly, I have no sense of humor. Were I in possession of such a gift, I would not be writing this tiresome memoir about my sexual life. Who cares? Who gives a rat's ass how many stems get inserted in my slot? It all adds up to nothing. Nothing but numbers, statistics worthy of a lecher's dusty ledger abandoned in an attic in a house in Rouen which no one visits, except for the groundskeeper, once a month – that is, if he remembers to show up and isn't too busy ramming his stem into somebody's slot.

Nine o'clock.

That's a literary device intended to kill time.

I've been standing in this line since seven and can't even make out the entrance in the distance. I'll consider myself fortunate if I ever get close enough to sniff the bouncer's crotch. I could devote half a page to describing what I cannot see… simply imagining what a bouncer's package looks like.

It's almost ten.

I suppose I could fuck and suck my way to the

front. "Mind if I cut in?" *Slurp.*

But then I'd be working the street and I'm *not* a prostitute. Besides, most of the men around me look like pigs. Not that it matters. What matters is an erect male member when one is writing a book such as this. I'm just thankful I'm writing this and not reading it – it would bore me to tears. I know that's a cliché, but nobody notices as long as there's plenty of action. That's what my editor, Alphonse, says. "Focus on the action, doll, and leave the emotions to Margaret Mitchell." I wrote that down because—like a good dildo—I knew I'd find a place to stick it.

It's after eleven.

Did someone say action?

I'm at a crossroads here. Unless you consider this erotic suspense.

Will she make it to the entrance? How long will it take her to get inside and get off? How many bodies will she get it on with? Will she be accosted by a dashing stranger? Will he take her away in a taxi? Will she sit on his face?

I think I'll write *Story of O* instead.

Shorter lines.

An Obscene Call by Nicholson Baker

"What are you wearing?" he asked.

She said, "I'm wearing white stockings with little stars, green and black stars, and sox the color of the green stars, and a pair of sox the color of the black stars, and a pair of heavy woolen ski-sox with little white snowmen, and one sock with yellow smiley faces and another with purple stripes, and blue bobby sox with a pretty pink floral pattern, and red ankle sox over a pair of brown nylons, and orange anklets with a Donald Duck motif, and a pair of white cotton sox with holes in the heels, and my ex-husband's tennis sox with horizontal red stripes and the name Nike, and also a Christmas stocking that my aunt gave me, and lime-green polyester boxing sox — heaven knows where they came from — a pair of red, white and blue sox with the Presidential seal on them, and some faded grey sweat sox that I should've washed months ago — ugh — and a pair of sox I found in the attic, they're black with white peace symbols, and —"

"—All right," he said. "Let me think about things. Let me absorb the strangeness."

"What's strange?"

"Nothing," he said. "I guess nothing. I think I should probably sign off now, though. I have to put a load of sox in the laundry."

"Okay. Well, thanks for calling, Bye, Jim."

"Jim?? This is Nick. Isn't this Abby?"

"No. This is Sheila."

"Oh ... I guess I have the wrong number. Bye, Sheila."

They hung up.

Body Talk

If the obscene is a matter of representation and not of sex, it must explore the very interior of the body and the viscera.

—Jean Baudrillard

Phase One

Mary found herself responding to Juan's caresses. An erective reaction occurred as the result of an involuntary contraction of muscular fibers within the structure of her nipples. Her left nipple became fully erect and tumescent, while the right one lagged in erective rapidity and tumescent size. The left nipple increased in length by .05 cm., while the base diameter grew by 0.25 cm.

"*Oh god,*" she sighed, clutching his ears for dear life.

Phase Two

A second physiologic alteration developed during the excitement phase: increased definition and extension of the venous patterns of her breasts. Yikes! —Engorgement of the vascular tree extended centrally nearly as far as the aureolus. As her excitement grew, there was a decided increase in the actual size of her breasts. This size increment resulted from the organs' deep vasocongestive reaction to Juan's advanced petting procedures (perfected while a high school student in Pasaic, NJ, c.2004). Even Juan noticed the pronounced engorgement in the lower or inferior portions of her pendulous breasts, the sight of which spurred him on to even bolder caresses.

She had not previously considered the protean character of her sex-flush reaction to Juan's effective sexual stimulation. The severity of the flush suggested that this experiment in foreplay might actually bring her to the forbidden *orgasmic phase*, a.k.a. "the Hesh-flash."

Phase Three

"Oh god ..." The maculopapular type of erythematous rash appeared now over the epigastrium. The flush spread rapidly over her breasts, first from the anterior surfaces and then on to the anterior chest wall. Both the lateral and the medial breast surfaces became involved, albeit a bit too enthusiastically, suggesting the premature approach of orgasm. Indeed, she and Juan watched wide-eyed as her sex flush spread over her lower abdomen, her shoulders, and even her *antecubital fossae*. "My sex flush has spread to my *antecubital fossae!*" she cried.

"Hunh?" said Juan

A measles-like rash broke out and spread over the anterior and lateral borders of her thighs, over her buttocks and her entire back. This was followed by a carpopedal spasm, a spastic contraction of the striated musculature of the hands and feet, resulting in an almost comic clutching response of her fingers and toes. Juan caught himself smiling mid-nip-tweak as she wrestled him to the floor with savage strength.

"Whoa there!" cried Juan, looking as if he had lost control of some heavy machinery. He was, however, unaware of the involuntary distention of Mary's external meatus. This dilation of the *urethral meatus* was of minimal degree, yet was accompanied by an urge to void. Perhaps, had he known this, he might have refrained from further stimulatory tactics. Mary complained to herself of pre-coital dysuria, and a high, firm perineum and nulliparous constriction of her vaginal outlet. Indeed, she feared she exhibited symptoms of "honeymoon cystitus," despite the fact that she hardly knew Juan. Was this due to a fluctuating cystocele and second-degree uterine descensus? Surely a constant level of residual urine had maintained its balance in her bladder – although her urge to void became understandable, albeit inexcusable, when considering her degree of excitement.

Phase Four

More mysterious a reaction was the voluntary contraction of Mary's external rectal sphincter. This stimulative technique seemed somewhat unnecessary prior to orgasmic release for the energy expended is redundant. Her contractions developed at 0.8-second intervals as Juan applied his tongue to her right nipple. She gritted her teeth, attempting to suppress the great urge to void upon Juan as he labored at her private parts.

Meanwhile, Juan was vaguely aware that Mary's heart rate had risen, yet he could not possibly have guessed the precise increase, from 110 to 186 beats per minute. So, too, was Juan ignorant of the elevations in Mary's systolic pressure from 30 to 80 mm. Such a cardiorespiratory response was not uncommon in young women, although Juan suspected that Mary was neurotic.

Mary, for her part, felt a sensation of excessive heat, for an involuntary perspiratory reaction had begun to develop. A filmy sheen of sweat appeared over her back, thighs, and anterior chest wall. Perspiration even ran from her axillae and became a visible surface coating on her entire body from shoulders to thighs.

Juan was sweating as well, and thus it was sometimes difficult to tell from whose body the various beads of perspiration had originated. A fair degree of involuntary drip-swap (cf. male flop sweat) is to be expected as sex tensions rise. At this point Mary's major labia began to thin out and flatten against her perineum. There was also a slight elevation of her labia in an upward and outward direction away from her vaginal outlet. This labial puffery and anterolateral elevation suggested that things were progressing smoothly, i.e., that this exercise was headed toward a full court coital press.

Now it was Mary's labia minora that began to respond with a marked expansion in diameter so that it protruded through the protective curtain of the thinning major labia, and in so doing was partially responsible for Mary's sudden cry of *"Oh migod .. !"* Furthermore, this increase in minor labial diameter added at least 1 cm. to the clinical length of Mary's vaginal barrel, with the one exception being the posterior wall of the vaginal outlet, also known as *No Man's Land,* which maintained the status quo, although an occasional echo could be heard from within the empty chamber.

Phase Five

Once the vasocongestive increase in diameter had been completed, a vivid color change occurred in the engorged minor labia, ranging from pink to a bright floral red. Juan noticed this "rainbow" effect on Mary's sex-skin and emitted an audible gasp, while maintaining his tongue manipulations on the area of her chest wall. As his own sexual tensions rose, there was a notable tensing and thickening of his scrotal integument, accomplished both by localized vasocongestion and by contraction of the smooth-muscle fibers of the dartos layer. Juan's previously unstimulated scrotal patterns of multiple folding and free movement were rapidly lost. The constriction of his scrotal integument produced a significant decrease in the internal diameter of his scrotal sac. There was also a marked restriction in free testicular movement in other than a perpendicular plane. As if that wasn't bad enough, his jeans were a size too small, adding to the pressure building at crotch-level.

"Ugh," groaned Juan, as his *constricted scrotal sac* **[Warning: do not attempt to rapidly repeat out loud the previous three italicized words]** With its resultant loss of internal diameter contributed secondary support to the reaction of testicular elevation during this advanced stage of the excitement phase.

His testes ascended toward the perineum and underwent a change in their axis of suspension during this process of elevation. The superior pole of Juan's ascending testes rotated anteriorly, and as a consequence, once elevated completely, his posterior testicular wall came in direct contact with his male perineum. As Juan well knew, the phenomenon of this pre-ejaculatory testicular elevation provided visible evidence of the physiologic intent of the well established clinical entity of the cremasteric reflex.

Sensing Juan's full testicular elevation, Mary wondered whether it was pathognomonic of an impending ejaculation. If so, it would clearly soil her new party dress and leave telltale evidence of their illicit exchange of bodily fluids. She glanced down at his left testicle to find it had not established complete perineal apposition.

"Thank god," sighed Mary. But her sense of relief was immediately disturbed by a series of contractions, commencing with the *vasa efferentia* of Juan's testes, and leading through the epididymus to the *vas deferens*. She watched closely, her mouth frozen in a grotesque grin, as his prostatic contractions palpitated in a mocking fashion that resembled her own previous pelvic and labial spasms. Was this Juan's way of letting her know he found her sex-flush and various responses ridiculous? Good lord, he hadn't even witnessed her convulsive, multiple-vagino-elastic-expulsive clitoral reactions yet.

Phase Six

Mary sat upright and commanded him to cease all carnal gestures. The surreality of the situation came to a grinding halt, as if a stage set had suddenly dissolved into an actual exterior street-scene in what is often referred to as "real life."

Juan stared dumbly at the ceiling, twiddled his bulbous thumbs, trying to appear nonchalant, as if this sudden disruption did not reflect poorly on his machismo-factor. Several moments passed as the couple sat in awkward silence, reflecting on their physiological adventures, wondering if indeed it had all been worth it. Finally, they stood erect and walked to the door.

"Goodbye," said Mary.

"I'll call ya sometime," said Juan, although he made no attempt to find out her last name.

It hardly mattered since both Juan and Mary had unlisted numbers.

DEREK PELL

Fifty Shades of Grey [*]

---

[*] AUTHOR'S NOTE: Even a satirist has to draw the line somewhere.

ABOUT THE AUTHOR

Derek Pell is a writer, visual artist, and photographer — the author of over 40 books, including works of experimental fiction, humor, satire, art and nonfiction. His work has appeared in some 300 newspapers and magazines in the U.S. and Europe, including *The London Times, L.A. Weekly, Village Voice, Rolling Stone, Interview, Natural History, Fiction International, National Lampoon,* and *The New York Times Sunday Magazine.*

Under his pseudonym Norman Conquest, he founded the international anti-censorship art collective, Beuyscouts of Amerika. He has produced works of mixed media, collage, book-objects, mail art, and multiple editions – several of which are part of the permanent collection of the Museum of Modern Art in NYC.

In 2012, he launched Black Scat Books (BlackScatBooks. com), a small independent press devoted to absurdist fiction, works in translation, and avant-garde art.

He lives at an undisclosed location in northern California with his wife and two large dogs.

A NOTE ON THE TYPE

This book has been set in Minion, a type designed by Robert Slimback in 1990. It derived from Slimback's development of Adobe Garamond, and is a contemporary face with its roots in the Renaissance.

Titles for the texts are set in Respective, created by Swedish designer Måns Grebäck. The exquisite script is ripe with flourishes and has a decidedly erotic aura.

The front cover's title type is a handcrafted mashup of Stereofidelic Regular and several other faces. The cover design mimics a British edition of Naked Lunch by William Burroughs, designed by Charles R. Woods.

Design & Composition by Norman Conquest

Other Great Works of Innovative Fiction Published by JEF Books

✦

Collected Stort Shories by Erik Belgum
Oppression for the Heaven of It by Moore Bowen [**2013 Patchen Award!**]
Don't Sing Aloha When I Go by Robert Casella
How to Break Article Noun by Carolyn Chun   [**2012 Patchen Award!**]
What Is Art? by Norman Conquest
Case X by James R. Hugunin
Elder Physics by James R. Hugunin
Something Is Crook in Middlebrook by James R. Hugunin [**2012
                    Zoom Street Experimental Fiction Book of the Year!**]
Tar Spackled Banner by James R. Hugunin
OD: Docufictions by Harold Jaffe
Othello Blues by Harold Jaffe
Paris 60 by Harold Jaffe
Apostrophe/Parenthesis by Frederick Mark Kramer
Ambiguity by Frederick Mark Kramer
Meanwhile by Frederick Mark Kramer
Minnows by Jønathan Lyons
You Are Make Very Important Bathtime by David Moscovich
Xanthous Mermaid Mechanics by Brion Poloncic
Return to Circa '96 by Bob Sawatzki   [**2014 Patchen Award!**]
Short Tails by Yuriy Tarnawsky
The Placebo Effect Trilogy by Yuriy Tarnawsky
Prism and Graded Monotony by Dominic Ward

For a complete listing of all our titles
please visit us at **experimentalfiction.com**